AUSTIN AND
HIS FRIENDS

AUSTIN AND HIS FRIENDS

JAMES H. BALFOUR

WILDSIDE PRESS

AUSTIN AND HIS FRIENDS

This edition published 2005 by Wildside Press, LLC.
www.wildsidepress.com

Chapter the First

It was rather a beautiful old house—the house where Austin lived. That is, it was old-fashioned, low-browed, solid, and built of that peculiar sort of red brick which turns a rich rose-colour with age; and this warm rosy tint was set off to advantage by the thick mantle of dark green ivy in which it was partly encased, and by the row of tall white and purple irises which ran along the whole length of the sunniest side of the building. There was an ancient sundial just above the door, and all the windows were made of small, square panes—not a foot of plateglass was there about the place; and if the rooms were nor particularly large or stately, they had that comfortable and settled look which tells of undisturbed occupancy by the same inmates for many years. But the principal charm of the place was the garden in which the house stood. In this case the frame was really more beautiful than the picture. On one side, the grounds were laid out in very formal style, with straight walks, clipped box hedges, an old stone fountain, and a perfect bowling-green of a lawn; while at right angles to this there was a plot of land in which all regularity was set at naught, and sweetpeas, tulips, hollyhocks, dahlias, gillyflowers, wallflowers, sunflowers, and a dozen others equally sweet and friendly shared the soil with gooseberry bushes and thriving apple trees. Taking it all in all, it was a lovable and most reposeful home, and Austin, who had lived there ever since he could remember, was quite unable to imagine any lot in life that could be compared to his.

Now this was curious, for Austin was a hopeless cripple. Up to the age of sixteen, he had been the most active, restless, healthy boy in all the countryside. He used to spend his days in boating, bicycling, climbing hills, and wandering at large through the woods and leafy lanes which stretched far and wide in all directions of the compass. One of his chief diversions had been sheep-chasing; nothing delighted him more than to start a whole flock of the astonished creatures careering madly round some broad green meadow, their fat woolly backs wobbling and jolting along in a compact mass of mild perplexity at this sudden interruption of their neverending meal, while Austin scampered at their tails, as much excited with the sport as Don Quixote himself when he dispersed the legions of Alifanfaron. Let hare-coursers, otter-hunters, and pigeon-torturers blame him if they choose; the exercise probably did the sheep a vast amount of good, and Austin fully believed that they enjoyed it quite as much as he did. Then suddenly a great calamity befell him. A weakness made itself apparent in his right knee, accompanied by considerable pain. The family doctor looked anxious and puzzled; a great surgeon was called in, and the two shook their heads together in very portentous style. It was a case of caries, they said, and Austin mustn't hunt sheep any more. Soon he had to lie upon the sofa for several hours a day, and what made Aunt Charlotte more anxious than anything else was that he didn't seem to mind lying on the sofa, as he would have done if he had felt strong and well; on the contrary, he grew thin and listless, and instead of always jumping up and trying to evade the doctor's orders, appeared quite content to lie there, quiet and resigned, from one week's end to another. That, thought shrewd Aunt Charlotte, betokened mischief. Another consultation followed, and then a very terrible sentence was pronounced. It was necessary, in order to save his life, that Austin should lose his leg.

What does a boy generally feel under such circumstances? What would you and I feel? Austin's first impulse was to burst into a passionate fit of weeping, and he yielded to it unreservedly. But, the fit once past, he smiled brilliantly through his tears. True, he would never again be able to enjoy those glorious ramps up hill and down dale that up till then had sent the warm life coursing through his veins. Never more would he go scorching along the level roads against the wind on his cherished bicycle. The open-air athletic days of stress and effort were gone, never to return. But there might be compensations; who could tell? Happiness, all said and done, need not depend upon a shinbone more or less. He might lose a leg, but legs were, after all, a mere concomitant to life—life did not consist in legs. There would still be something left to live for, and who could tell whether that something might not be infinitely grander and nobler and more satisfying than even the rapture of flying ten miles an hour on his wheel, or chevying a flock of agitated sheep from one pasture to another?

Where this sudden inspiration came from, he then had no idea; but come it did, in the very nick of time, and helped him to dry his tears. The day of destiny also came, and his courage was put to the test. He knew well enough, of course, that of the operation he would feel nothing. But the sight of the hard, white, narrow pallet on which he had to lie, the cold glint of the remorseless instruments, the neatly folded packages of lint and cotton-wool, and the faint, horrible smell of chloroform turned him rather sick for a minute. Then he glanced downwards, with a sense of almost affectionate yearning, at the limb he was about to lose. "Good-bye, dear old leg!" he murmured, with a little laugh which smothered a rising sob. "We've had some lovely ramps together, but the best of friends must part."

Afterwards, during the long days of dreary convalescence, he began to feel an interest in what remained of it; and then he found himself taking a sort of æsthetic pleasure in the smooth, beautifully-rounded stump, which really was in its way quite an artistic piece of work. At last, when the flesh was properly healed, and the white skin growing healthily again around his abbreviated member, he grew eager to make acquaintance with his new leg; for of course it was never intended that he should perform the rest of his earthly pilgrimage with only a leg and a half—let the added half be of what material it might. And his excitement may be better imagined than described when, one afternoon, the surgeon came in with a most wonderful object in his arms—a lovely prop of bright, black, burnished wood, set off with steel couplings and the most fascinating straps you ever saw. And the best of all was the socket, in which his soft white stump fitted as comfortably as though they had been made for one another—as, in fact, one of them had been. It was a little difficult to walk just at first, for Austin was accustomed to begin by throwing out his foot, whereas now he had to begin by moving his thigh; this naturally made him stagger, and for some time he could only get along with the aid of a crutch. But to be able to walk again at all was a great achievement, and then, if you only looked at it in the proper light, it really was great fun.

There was, however, one person who, probably from a defective sense of humour, was unable to see any fun in it at all. Aunt Charlotte would have given her very ears for Austin, but her affection was of a somewhat irritable sort, and generally took the form of scolding. She was not a stupid woman by any means, but there was one thing in the world she never could understand, and that was Austin himself. He wasn't like other boys one bit, she always said. He had such a queer, topsy-turvy way of looking at things; would express the most outrageous opinions with an innocent unconsciousness that made her long to box his ears, and support the most arrant absurdities by arguments that conveyed not the smallest meaning to her intellect. Look at him now, for instance; a cripple for life, and pretending to see nothing in it but a joke, and expressing as much admiration for his horrible wooden leg as though it had been a king's sceptre! In Aunt Charlotte's view, Austin ought to have pitied himself immensely, and expressed a hope that God would help him to bear his burden with orthodox resignation to the Divine will; instead of which, he seemed totally unconscious of having any burden at all—a state of mind that was nothing less than impious. Austin was now seventeen, and it was high time that he took more serious views of life. Ever since he was a baby he had been her special charge; for his mother had died in giving him birth, and his father had followed her about a twelvemonth later. She had always done her duty to the boy, and loved him as though he had been her own; but she reminded onlookers rather of a conscientious elderly cat with limited views of natural history condemned by circumstances to take care of a very irresponsible young eaglet. The eaglet, on his side, was entirely devoted to his protectress, but it was impossible for him not to feel a certain lenient and amused contempt for her very limited horizon.

"Auntie," he said to her one day, "you're just like a frog at the bottom of a well. You think the speck of blue you see above you is the entire sky, and the water you paddle up and down in is the ocean. Why can't you take a rather more cosmic view of things?"

This extraordinary remark occurred in the course of a wrangle between the two, because Austin insisted on his pet cat—a plump, white, matronly creature he had christened 'Gioconda,' because (so *he* said) she always smiled so sweetly—sitting up at the dinner-table and being fed with tit-bits off his own fork; and Aunt Charlotte objected to this proceeding on the ground that the proper place for cats was in the kitchen. Austin, on his side, averred that cats were in many ways much superior to human beings; that they had been worshipped as gods by the philosophical Egyptians because they were so scornful and mysterious; and that Gioconda herself was not only the divinest cat alive, but entitled to respect, if only as an embodiment and representative of cat-hood in the abstract, which was a most important element in the economy of the universe. It was when Aunt Charlotte stigmatised these philosophical reflections as a pack of impertinent twaddle that Austin had had the audacity to say that she was like a frog.

And now her eaglet had been maimed for life, and whatever he might feel about it himself her own responsibilities were certainly much increased. At this very moment, for instance, after having practised stumping about the room for half an hour he insisted on going downstairs. Of course the idea was ridiculous. Even the doctor shook his head, while old Martha, who had tubbed Austin when he was two years old, joined in the general protest. But Austin, disdaining to argue the point with any one of them, had already hobbled out of the room, and before they were well aware of it had begun to essay the descent perilous. Ominous bumps were heard, and then a dull thud as of a body falling. But a bend in the wall had caught the body, and the explorer was none the worse. Then Aunt Charlotte, rushing back into the bedroom, flung open the window wide.

"Lubin!" she shouted lustily.

A young gardener boy, tall, round-faced and curly-haired, glanced up astonished from his work among the sweetpeas.

"Come up here directly and carry Master Austin downstairs. He's got a wooden leg and hasn't learnt how to use it."

The consequence of which was that two minutes later Austin, panting and enraged at the failure of his first attempt at independence, found himself firmly encircled by a pair of strong young arms, lifted gently from the ground, and carried swiftly and safely downstairs and out at the garden door.

"Now you just keep quiet, Master Austin," murmured Lubin, chuckling as Austin began to kick. "No use your starting to run before you know how to walk. Wooden legs must be humoured a bit, Sir; 'twon't do to expect too much of 'em just at first, you see. This one o' yours is mighty handsome to look at, I don't deny, but it's not accustomed to staircases and maybe it'll take some time before it is. Hold tight, Sir; only a few yards more now. There! Here we are on the lawn at last. Now you can try your paces at your leisure."

"You're awfully nice to me, Lubin," gasped Austin, red with mortification, as he slipped from the lad's arms on to the grass, "but I felt just now as if I could have killed you, all the same."

"Lor', Sir, I don't mind," said Lubin. "I doubt that was no more'n natural. Can you stand steady? Here—lay hold o' my arm. Slow and sure's the word. Look out for that flowerbed. Now, then, round you go—that's it. Ah!"—as Austin fell sprawling on the grass. "Now how are you going to get up again, I should like to know? Seems to me the first thing you've got to learn is not to lose your balance, 'cause once you're down 'tain't the easiest thing in creation to scramble up again. You'll have to stick to the crutch at first, I reckon. Up we come! Now let's see how you can fare along a bit all by yourself."

Austin was thankful for the support of his crutch, with the aid of which he managed to stagger about for a few minutes at quite a respectable speed. It reminded him almost of the far-off days when he was learning to ride his bicycle. At last he thought he would like to rest a bit, and was much surprised when, on flinging himself down upon a garden seat, his leg flew up in the air.

"Lively sort o' limb, this new leg o' yours, Sir," commented Lubin, as he bent it into a more decorous position. "You'll have to take care it don't carry you off with it one o' these fine days. Seems to me it wants taming, and learning how to behave itself in company. I heard tell of a cork leg once upon a time as was that nimble it started off running on its own account, and no earthly power could stop it. Wouldn't have mattered so much if it'd had nobody but itself to consider, but unluckily the gentleman it belonged to happened to be screwed on to the top end of it, and of course he had to follow. They do say as how he's following it still—poor beggar! Must be worn to a shadow by this time, I should think. But p'raps it ain't true after all. There are folks as'll say anything."

"I expect it's true enough," replied Austin cheerfully. "If you want a thing to be true, all you've got to do is to believe it—believe it as hard as you can. That makes it true, you see. At least, that's what the new psychology teaches. Thought creates things, you understand—though how it works I confess I can't explain. But never mind. Oh, dear, how drunk I am!"

"Drunk, Sir? No, no, only a bit giddy," said Lubin, as he stood watching Austin with his hands upon his hips. "You're not over strong yet, and that new leg of yours has been giving you too much exercise to begin with. You just keep quiet a few minutes, and you'll soon be as right as ninepence."

Then Austin slid carefully off the seat, and stretched himself full length upon the grass. "I *am* drunk," he murmured, closing his eyes, "drunk with the scent of the flowers. Don't you smell them, Lubin? The air's heavy with it, and it has got into my brain. And how sweet the grass smells too. I love it—it's like breathing the breath of Nature. What do legs matter? It's much nicer to roll over the grass wherever you want to go than to have the bother of walking. Don't worry about me any more, nice Lubin. Go on tying up your sweetpeas. I'll come and help you when I'm tired of rolling about. Just now I don't want anything; I'm drunk—I'm happy—I'm satisfied—I'm happier than I ever was before. Be kind to the flowers, Lubin; don't tie them too tight. They're my friends and my lovers. Aren't you a little fond of them too?"

Then, left to his own reflections, he lay perfectly peaceful and content staring up into the sky. For months he had been fated to lead an entirely new life, and now it had actually begun. His entrance upon it was not bitter. He had flowers growing by his path, and books that he loved, and one or two friends who loved him. It was all right! And that was how he spent his first day of acknowledged cripplehood.

Chapter the Second

In a very short time Austin had overcome the initial difficulties of locomotion, and now began to take regular exercise out of doors. It would be too much to say that his gait was particularly elegant; but there really was something triumphal about the way in which he learnt to brandish his leg with every step he took, and the majestic swing with which he brought it round to its place in advance of the other. In fact, he soon found himself stumping along the highroads with wonderful speed and safety; though to clamber over stiles, and work a bicycle one-footed, of course took much more practice.

Hitherto I have said nothing about the neighbourhood of Austin's home. Now when I say neighbourhood, I don't mean the topographical surroundings—I use the word in its correcter sense of neighbours; and these it is necessary to refer to in passing. Of course there were several people living round about. There was the MacTavish family, for instance, consisting of Mr and Mrs MacTavish, five daughters and two sons. Mrs MacTavish had a brother who had been knighted, and on the strength of such near relationship to Sir Titus and Lady Clandougal, considered herself one of the county. But her claim was not endorsed, even by the humbler gentry with whom she was forced to associate, while as for the county proper it is not too much to say that that august community had never even heard of her. The Miss MacTavishes, ranging in age from fifteen to five-and-twenty, were rather gawky young persons, with red hair and a perpetual giggle; in fact they could not speak without giggling, even if it was to tell you that somebody was dead. Every now and then Mrs MacTavish would proclaim, with portentous complacency, that Florrie, or Lizzie, or Aggie, was "out"—to the awestruck admiration of her friends; which meant that the young person referred to had begun to do up her hair in a sort of bun at the back of her head, and had had her frock let down a couple of tucks. Austin couldn't bear them, though he was always scrupulously polite. And the boys were, if anything, less interesting than the girls. The elder of the two—a freckled young giant named Jock—was always asking him strange conundrums, such as whether he was going to put the pot on for the Metropolitan—which conveyed no more idea to Austin's mind than if he had said it in Chinese; while Sandy, the younger, used to terrify him out of his wits by shouting out that Yorkshire had got the hump, or that Jobson was 'not out' for a century, or that wickets were cheap at the Oval. In fact, the entire family bored him to extinction, though Aunt Charlotte, who had been an old school-friend of the mamma, sang their praises perseveringly, and said that the girls were dears.

Then there was the inevitable vicar, with a wife who piqued herself on her smart bonnets; a curate, who preached Socialism, wore knickerbockers, and belonged to the Fabian Society; a few unattached elderly ladies who had long outlived the reproach of their virginity; and just two or three other families with nothing particular to distinguish them one way or another. It may readily be inferred, therefore, that Austin had not many associates. There was really no one in the place who interested him in the very least, and the consequence was that he was generally regarded as unsociable. And so he was—very unsociable. The companionship of his books, his bicycle, his flowers and his thoughts was far more precious to him than that of the silly people who bothered him to join in their vapid diversions and unseasonable talk, and he rightly acted upon his preference. His own resources were of such a nature that he never felt alone; and having but few comrades in the flesh, he wisely courted the society of those whom, though long since dead, he held in far higher esteem than all the elderly ladies and curates and MacTavishes who ever lived. His appetite in literature was keen, but fastidious. He devoured all the books he could procure about the Renaissance of art in Italy. The works of Mr Walter Pater were as a treasure-house of suggestion to him, and did much to form and guide his gradually developing mentality. He read Plato, being even more fascinated by the exquisite technique of the dialectic than by the ethical value of the teaching. And there was one small, slim book that he always carried about with him, and kept for special reading in the fields and woods. This was Virgil's Eclogues, the sylvan atmosphere of which penetrated the very depths of his being, and created in him a moral or spiritual atmosphere which was its counterpart. He seemed to live amid gracious pastoral scenes, where beautiful youths and maidens passed a perpetual springtime in a land of dewy lawns, and shady groves, and pools, and rippling streams. Daphnis and Mopsus, Corydon, Alexis, and Amyntas, were all to him real personages, who peopled his solitude, inspired his poetic fancy, and fostered in his imagination the elements of an ideal life where the beauty and purity and freshness of untainted Nature reigned supreme. The accident of his lameness, by incapacitating him for violent exer-

cise out of doors, ministered to the development of this spiritual
tendency, and threw him back upon the allurements of a refined
idealism. Daphnis became to him the embodiment, the concrete
image, of eternal youthhood, of adolescence in the abstract, the
attribute of an idealised humanity. To lead the pure Daphnis life
of simplicity, stainlessness, communion with beautiful souls, was
to lead the highest life. To find one's bliss in sunshine, flowers,
and the winds of heaven—in both the physical and moral
spheres—was to find the highest bliss. Why should not he, Austin
Trevor, cripple as he was, so live the Daphnis life as to be himself
a Daphnis?

No wonder a boy like this was voted unsociable. No wonder
Sandy and Jock despised him as a muff, and the young ladies
deplored his unaccountably elusive ways. The truth was that
Austin simply had no use for any of them; his life was complete
without them, it contained no niche into which they could ever fit.
Lubin was a far more congenial comrade. Lubin never bothered
him about football, or cricket, or horseracing, never worried him
with invitations to horrible picnics, never outraged his sensibilities in any way. On the contrary, Lubin rather contributed to his
happiness by the care he took of the flowers, and the intelligence
he showed in carrying out all Austin's elaborately conveyed
instructions. Why, Lubin himself was a sort of Daphnis—in a
humble way. But Sandy! No, Austin was not equal to putting up
with Sandy.

There was, however, one gentleman in the neighbourhood
whom Master Austin was gracious enough to approve. This was a
certain Mr Roger St Aubyn, a man of taste and culture, who possessed a very rare collection of fine pictures and old engravings
which nobody had ever seen. St Aubyn was, in fact, something of a
recluse, a student who seldom went beyond his park gates, and
found his greatest pleasure in reading Greek and cultivating
orchids. It was by the purest accident that the two came across
each other. Austin was lying one afternoon on a bank of wild hyacinths just outside Combe Spinney, lazily admiring the effect of
his bright black leg against the bright blue sky, and thinking of
nothing in particular. Mr St Aubyn, who happened to be strolling
in that direction, was attracted by the unwonted spectacle, and
ventured on some good-humoured quizzical remark. This led to a
conversation, in the course of which the scholar thought he discovered certain original traits in the modest observations of the
youth. One topic drifted into another, and soon the two were
engaged in an animated discussion about pursuits in life. It was

in the course of this that Austin let drop the one word—Art.

"What is Art?" queried St Aubyn.

Austin hesitated for some moments. Then he said, very slowly:

"That is a question to which a dozen answers might be given. A whole book would be required to deal with it."

St Aubyn was delighted, both at the reply and at the hesitation that had preceded it.

"And are you an artist?" he enquired.

"I believe I am," replied Austin, very seriously. "Of course one doesn't like to be too confident, and I can't draw a single line, but still——"

"Good again," approved the other. "Here as in everything else all depends upon the definition. What is an artist?"

"An artist," exclaimed Austin, kindling, "is one who can see the beauty everywhere."

"*The* beauty?" repeated St Aubyn.

"The beauty that exists everywhere, even in ugly things. The beauty that ordinary people don't see," returned Austin. "Anybody can see beauty in what are *called* beautiful things—light, and colour, and grace. But it takes an artist to see beauty in a muddy road, and dripping branches, and drenching rain. How people cursed and grumbled on that rainy day we had last week; it made me sick to hear them. Now I saw the beauty *under* the ugliness of it all—the wonderful soft greys and browns, the tiny glints of silver between the leaves, the flashes of pearl and orpiment behind the shifting clouds. Do you know, I even see beauty in this wooden leg of mine, great beauty, though everybody else thinks it perfectly hideous! So that is why I hope I am not wrong in imagining that perhaps I may, really, be in some sense an artist."

For a moment St Aubyn did not speak. "The boy's a great artist," he muttered to himself. His interest was now excited in good earnest; here was no common mind. Of art Austin knew practically nothing, but the artistic instinct was evidently tingling in every vein of him. St Aubyn himself lived for art and literature, and was amazed to have come across so curiously exceptional a personality. He drew the boy out a little more, and then, in a moment of impulse, did a most unaccustomed thing: he invited Austin to lunch with him on the following Thursday, promising, in addition, that they should spend the afternoon together looking over his conservatories and picture-gallery.

So great an honour, so undreamt-of a privilege, sent Austin's blood to the roots of his hair. He flourished his leg more proudly than ever as he stumped victoriously home and announced the great news to Aunt Charlotte. That estimable lady was fingering some notepaper on her writing-table as her excited nephew came bursting in upon her with his face radiant.

"Auntie," he cried, "what do you think? You'll never guess. I'm going to lunch with Mr St Aubyn on Thursday!"

Aunt Charlotte turned round, looking slightly dazed.

"Going to lunch with whom?" she asked.

"With Mr St Aubyn. You know—he lives at Moorcombe Court. I met him in the woods and had a long talk with him, and now he's going to show me all his pictures—*and* his engravings—*and* his wonderful orchids and things. I'm to spend all the afternoon with him. Isn't it splendid! I could never have hoped for such an opportunity. And he's so awfully nice—so cultured and clever, you know—"

"Really!" said Aunt Charlotte, drawing herself up. "Well, you're vastly honoured, Austin, I must say. Mr St Aubyn is chary of his civilities. It is very kind of him to ask you, I'm sure, but I think it's rather a liberty all the same."

"A liberty!" repeated Austin, aghast.

"He has never called on me," returned Aunt Charlotte, statelily. "If he had wished to cultivate our acquaintance, that would have been at least the usual thing to do. However, of course I've no objection. On Thursday, you say. Well, now just give me your attention to something rather more important. I intend to invite some people here to tea next week, and you may as well write the invitations for me now."

Austin's face lengthened. "Oh, why?" he sighed. "It isn't as though there was anybody worth asking—and really, the horrid creatures that infest this neighbourhood—. Whom do you want to ask?"

"I'm astonished at you, speaking of our friends like that," replied his aunt, severely. "They're not horrid creatures; they're all very nice and kind. Of course we must have the MacTavishes——"

"I knew it," groaned Austin, sinking into a chair. "Those dear MacTavishes! There are nineteen of them, aren't there? Or is it only nine?"

"Don't be ridiculous, Austin," said Aunt Charlotte. "Then there are the Miss Minchins—that'll be eleven; the vicar and his wife, of *course*; and old Mr and Mrs Cobbledick. Now just come and sit here——"

"The Cobbledicks—those old murderers!" cried Austin. "Do

you want us to be all assassinated together?"

"Murderers!" exclaimed Aunt Charlotte, horrified. "I think you've gone out of your mind. A dear kindly old couple like the Cobbledicks! Not very handsome, perhaps, but—murderers! What in the world will you say next?"

"The most sinister-looking old pair of cutthroats in the parish," returned Austin. "I should be sorry to meet them on a lonely road on a dark night, I know that. But really, auntie, I do wish you'd think better of all this. We're quite happy alone; what do we want of all these horrible people coming to bore us for Heaven knows how many hours? Of course I shall be told off to amuse the MacTavishes; just think of it! Seven red-haired, screaming, giggling monsters——"

"Hold your tongue, do, you abominable boy!" cried Aunt Charlotte. "I'm inviting our friends for *my* pleasure, not for yours, and I forbid you to speak of them in that wicked, slanderous, disrespectful way. Come now, sit down here and write me the invitations at once."

"For the last time, auntie, I entreat you——" began Austin.

"Not a word more!" replied his aunt. "Begin without more ado."

"Well, if you insist," consented Austin, as he dragged himself into the seat. "Have you fixed upon a day?"

"No—any day will do. Just choose one yourself," said Aunt Charlotte, as she dived after an errant ball of worsted. "What day will suit you best?"

"Shall we say the 24th?" suggested Austin.

"By all means," replied his aunt briskly. "If you're sure that that won't interfere with anything else. I've such a wretched memory for dates. Today is the 19th. Yes, I should say the 24th will do very well indeed."

"It will suit me admirably," said Austin, sitting down and beginning to write with great alacrity, while his aunt busied herself with her knitting. As soon as the envelopes were addressed, he slipped them into his coat pocket, and, rising, said he might as well go out and post them there and then.

"Do," said Aunt Charlotte, well pleased at Austin's sudden capitulation. "That is, unless you're too tired with your walk. Martha can always give them to the milkman if you are."

"Not a bit of it," said Austin hastily, as he swung himself out of the room. "I shall be back in time for dinner."

"He certainly is the very oddest boy," soliloquised Aunt Charlotte, as she settled herself comfortably on the sofa and went on clicking her knitting-needles. "Why he dislikes the MacTavishes so I can't imagine; nice, cheerful young persons as anyone would wish to see. It really is very queer. And then the way he suddenly gave in at last! It only shows that I must be firm with him. As soon as he saw I was in earnest he yielded at once. He's got a sweet nature, but he requires a firm hand. He's different, too, since he lost his leg—more full of fancies, it seems to me, and a great deal too much wrapped up in those books of his. I suppose that when one's body is defective, one's mind feels the effects of it. I shall have to keep him up to the mark, and see that he has plenty of cheerful society. Nothing like nice companions for maintaining the brain in order."

Thus did Aunt Charlotte decide to her own satisfaction what she thought would be best for Austin.

Chapter the Third

He stood leaning against the old stone fountain on the straight lawn under the noonday sun. The bees hummed slumberously around him, sailing from flower to flower, and the hot air, laden with the scents of the soil, seemed to penetrate his body at every pore, infusing a sense of vitality into him which pulsed through all his veins. Austin always said that high noon was the supreme moment of the day. To some folks the most beautiful time was dawn, to others sunset, but at noon Nature was like a flower at its full, a flower in the very zenith of its strength and glory. He had always loved the noon.

"The world seems literally palpitating with life," he thought, as he rested his arm on the rim of the timeworn fountain. "I'm sure it's conscious, in some way or other. How it must enjoy itself! Look at the trees; so strong, and calm, and splendid. They know well enough how strong they are, and when there's a storm that tries to blow them down, how they do revel in battling with it! And then the hot air, embracing the earth so voluptuously—playing with the slender plants, and caressing the upstanding flowers. They stand up because they want to be caressed, the amorous creatures. How wonderful it is—the different characters that flowers have. Some are shrill and fierce and passionate, while others are meek and sly, and pretend to shrink when they are even noticed. Some are wicked—shamelessly, insolently, magnificently wicked—like those scarlet anthuriums, with their curling yellow tongues. That flower is the very incarnation of sin; no, not incarnation—what's the word? I can't think, but it doesn't matter. Incarnation will do, for the thing is exactly like recalcitrant human flesh. Lubin!"

"Yes, Sir?" responded Lubin, who was digging near.

"What are the wickedest flowers you know?" asked Austin.

"Well, Sir, I should say them as had most thorns," said Lubin feelingly.

"I wonder," mused Austin. Then he relapsed into his meditations. "How thick with life the air is. I'm sure it's populated, if we only had eyes to see. I feel it throbbing all round me—full of beings as much alive as I am, only invisible. People used to see them once upon a time—why can't we now? Naiads, and dryads, and fauns, and the great god Pan everywhere; oh, to think we may be actually surrounded by these wonders of beauty, and yet unable to talk to any of them! Nothing but wicked old women, and horrible young men in plaid knickerbockers and bowler hats, who worry one about odds and handicaps. It's all very sad and ugly."

"Aren't you rather hot, standing there in the sun, Sir, all this time?" said Lubin, looking up.

"Very hot," replied Austin. "I wonder what time it is?"

Lubin glanced up at the sundial. "Just five minutes past the hour, or thereabouts, I make it."

"Oh, Lubin, let's go and bathe!" cried Austin suddenly. "You must be far hotter than I am. There's plenty of time—we don't lunch till half past one. How long would it take us to get to the bathing-pool just at the bend of the river?"

"Well—not above ten minutes, I should say," was Lubin's answer. "I'd like a dip myself more'n a little, but I'm not quite sure if I ought to—you see the mistress wants all this finished up by the afternoon, and then——"

"But you must!" insisted Austin. "You forget that I've only got one leg, so I can't swim as I used, and you've got to come and take care I don't get drowned. 'O weep for Adonais—he is dead!' How angry Aunt Charlotte would be. And then she'd cry, poor dear, and go into hideous mourning for her poor Austin. Come along, Lubin—but wait, I must just go and get a couple of towels. Oh, I'm simply mad for the water. I'll be back in less than a flash."

Lubin drove his spade into the earth, turned down his sleeves, and rested—a fair-skinned, bronzed, wholesome object, good to look at—while Austin stumped away. In less than five minutes the two youths started off together, tramping through the long, lush meadow-grass which lay between the end of the garden and the river. The sun burned fiercely overhead, and the air quivered in the heat.

"Isn't it wonderful!" cried Austin, when they reached the edge of the water, and were standing under the shade of some trees that overhung the towing-path. "Come, Lubin, strip—I'm half undressed already. Look at the white and purple lights in the water—aren't they marvellous? Now we're going right down into them. Oh the freedom of air, and colour, and body—how I do *hate* clothes! I say, how funny my stump looks, doesn't it? Just like a great white rolling-pin. You must go in first, Lubin, and then you'll be prepared to catch me when I begin drowning."

Lubin, standing nude and shapely, like a fair Greek statue, for a moment on the bank, took a silent header and disappeared. Then Austin prepared to follow. He tumbled rather than plunged into the water, and, unable to attain an erect position owing to his imperfect organism, would have fared badly if Lubin had not caught him in his arms and turned him deftly over on his back.

"You just content yourself with floating face upwards, Sir," he said. "There's no sort of use in trying to strike out, you'd only sink to the bottom like a boat with a hole in it. There—let me hold you like this; one hand'll do it. Look out for the river-weeds. Now try and work your foot. Seems to be making you go round and round, somehow. But that don't matter. A bathe's a bathe, all said and done. How jolly cool it is!"

"Isn't it exquisite?" murmured Austin, with closed eyes. "I do think that drowning must be a lovely death. We're like the min-nows, Lubin, 'staying their wavy bodies 'gainst the streams, to taste the luxury of sunny beams tempered with coolness.' That's what *our* wavy bodies are doing now. Don't you like it? 'Now more than ever it seems rich to die——'"

But the next moment, owing probably to Lubin having lost his equilibrium, the young rhapsodist found himself, spluttering and half choked, nearer to the bed of the river than the surface, while his leg was held in chancery by a network of clinging water-weeds. Lubin had some slight difficulty in extricating him, and for the moment, at least, his poetic fantasies came to an abrupt and unromantic finish.

"Here, get on my back, and I'll swim you out as far as them waterlilies," said Lubin, giving him a dexterous hoist. "I'm aw-fully keen on the yellow sort, and they look wonderful fine ones. That's better. Now, Sir, you can just imagine yourself any drownded heathen as comes into your head, only hold tight and don't stir. If you do you'll get drownded in good earnest, and I shall have to settle accounts with your aunt afterwards. Are you ready? Right, then. And now away we go."

He struck out strongly and slowly, with Austin crouching on his shoulders. They arrived in safety at the point aimed at, and managed to tear away a grand cluster of the great, beautiful yellow flowers; but the process was a very ticklish one, and the struggle resulted, not unnaturally, in Austin becoming dislodged from his not very secure position, and floundering head foremost into the depths. Lubin caught him as he rose again, and, taking him firmly by one hand, helped him to swim alongside of him back to the shore. It was a difficult feat, and by the time they had accomplished the distance they were both pretty well exhausted.

"You *have* been good to me, Lubin," gasped Austin, as he flung himself sprawling on the grass. "I've had a lovely time—haven't you too? Was I very heavy? Perhaps it is rather a bore to have only one leg when one wants to swim. But now you can always say you've saved me from drowning, can't you. I should have gone under a dozen times if you hadn't held me up and lugged me about. Oh, dear, now we must put on our clothes again—what a barbarism clothes are! I do hate them so, don't you? But I suppose there's no help for it.

"Rise, Lubin, rise, and twitch thy mantle blue;
Tomorrow to fresh woods, and pastures new.

"Oh, do help me to screw on my leg. That's it. I say, it's a quarter-past one! We must hurry up, or Aunt Charlotte will be cursing. What *does* it matter if one eats at half past one or at a quarter to two? I really am very fond of Aunt Charlotte, you know, though I find it awfully difficult to educate her. I sometimes despair of ever being able to bring her up properly at all, she is so hopelessly Early Victorian, poor thing. But, then, so many people are, aren't they? Now animals are never Early Victorian; that's why I respect them so. If you weren't a human being, Lubin—and a very nice one, as you are—what sort of an animal would you like to be?"

"Well, I don't rightly know as I ever considered the point," said Lubin, passing his fingers through his drenched curls. "Perhaps I'd as lief be a squirrel as anything. I'm awfully fond o' nuts, and when I was a kid I used to spend half my time a-climbing trees. A squirrel must have rather a jolly life of it, when one comes to think."

"What a splendid idea!" cried Austin, as they prepared to start. "You *are* clever, Lubin. It would be lovely to live in a tree, curtained all round with thousands of quivering green leaves. I wish I knew what animals think about all day. It must be very dull for them never to have any thoughts, poor dears, and yet they seem happy enough somehow. Perhaps they have something else instead to make up for it—something that we've no idea of. I *say*—it's half past one!"

So Austin was late for lunch after all, and got a scolding from Aunt Charlotte, who told him that it was exceedingly ill-bred to inconvenience other people by habitual unpunctuality. Austin was very penitent, and promised he'd never be unpunctual again if he lived to be a hundred. Then Aunt Charlotte was mollified, and regaled him with an improving account of a most excellent book she had just been reading, upon the importance of instilling sound principles of political economy into the mind of the agricultural labourer. It was so essential, she explained, that people in that position should understand something about the laws which govern prices, the relations of capital and labour, the *metayer* system, and the ratio which should exist between an increase of population and the exhaustion of the soil by too frequent crops of wheat; and she wound up by propounding a series of hypothetical problems based on the doctrines she had set forth, for Austin to solve offhand.

Austin listened very dutifully for some time, but the subject bored him atrociously, and his attention began to wander. At last he made some rather vague and irrelevant replies, and then announced boldly that he thought all politicians were very silly old gentlemen, particularly economists; for his own part, he hated economy, especially when he wanted to buy something beautiful to look at; he further considered that political economists would be much better employed if they sat contemplating tulips instead of writing horrid books, and that Lubin was a great deal wiser than the whole pack of them put together. Then Aunt Charlotte got extremely angry, and a great wrangle ensued, in the course of which she said he was a foolish, ignorant boy, who talked nonsense for the sake of talking it. Austin replied by asking if she knew what a quincunx was, or what Virgil was really driving at when he composed the First Eclogue, and whether she had ever heard of Lycidas; and when she said that she had something better to do than stuff her head with quidnunxes and all such pagan rubbish, he remarked very politely that ignorance was evidently not all of the same sort. Which sent Aunt Charlotte bustling away in a huff to look after her household duties.

"It's all very sad and very ugly, isn't it, Gioconda?" sighed Austin, as he lifted the large, white, fluffy animal upon his lap. "You're a great philosopher, my dear; I wish I were as wise as you. You're so scornful, so dignified, so divinely egoistic. But you don't mind being worshipped, do you, Gioconda? Because you know it's your right, of course. There—she's actually condescending to purr! Now we'll come and disport ourselves under the trees, and you shall watch the birds from a safe distance. I know your wicked ways, and I must teach you how to treat your inferiors with proper benignity and toleration."

But Gioconda had plans of her own for the afternoon, and declined the proposed discipline; so Austin strolled off by himself, and lay down under the trees with a large book on Italian gardens to console him. His improvised exertions in the water had produced a certain fatigue, and he felt lazy and inert. Gradually he dropped off into a doze, which lasted more than an hour. And he had a curious dream. He thought he was in some strange land—a land like a garden seen through yellow glass—where everything was transparent, and people glided about as though they were skating, without any conscious effort. Then Aunt Charlotte appeared upon the scene, and he saw by her eyes that she was very angry because Lycidas had been drowned while bathing; but Austin assured her that it was Lubin who was drowned, and that it really was of no consequence, because Lubin was only a squirrel after all. At this point things got extremely mixed, and the sound of voices broke in upon his slumbers. He opened his eyes, and saw Aunt Charlotte herself in the act of walking away with a toss of her head that betokened a ruffled temper.

Austin's interest was immediately aroused. "Lubin!" he called softly, motioning the lad to come nearer. "What was she rowing you about? Was she blowing you up about this morning?"

"Well," confessed Lubin with a broad smile, "she didn't seem over-pleased. Said you might have lost your life, going out o' your depth with only one leg to stand on, and that if you'd been drownded I should have had to answer for it before a judge and jury."

"What a wicked, abandoned old woman!" cried Austin. "Only one leg to stand on, indeed!—she hasn't a single leg to stand on when she says such things. She ought to have gone down on her knees and thanked you for taking such care of me. But I shall never make anything of her, I'm afraid. The more I try to educate her the worse she gets."

"I shouldn't wonder," replied Lubin sagely. "The old hen feels herself badly off when the egg teaches her to cackle. That's human nature, that is. And then she was riled because she was afraid I shouldn't have time to get the garden-things in order by tomorrow, when it seems there's some sort o' company expected. I told her 'twould be all right."

"Oh, those brutes! Of course, they're coming tomorrow. I'd nearly forgotten all about it. It's just like Aunt Charlotte to be so fond of all those hideous people. You hate the MacTavishes, don't you, Lubin? *Do* hate the MacTavishes! Fancy—nine of them, no less, counting the old ones, and all of them coming together. What a family! I despise people who breed like rabbits, as though they thought they were so superlative that the rest of the world could never have enough of them."

"Ay, fools grow without watering," assented Lubin. "Can't say I ever took to 'em myself—though it's not my place to say so.

The young gents make a bit too free with one, and when they opens their mouths no one else may so much as sneeze. Think they know everything, they do. There's a saying as I've heard, that asses sing badly 'cause they pitch their voices too high. Maybe it's the same wi' them."

"Well, I hope Aunt Charlotte will enjoy their conversation," said Austin comfortably. "I say, Lubin, do you know anything about a Mr St Aubyn, who lives not far from here?"

"What, him at the Court?" replied Lubin. "I don't know him myself, but they say as *he's* a gentleman, and no mistake. Keeps himself to himself, he does, and has always got a civil word for everybody. Fine old place, too, that of his."

"Have you ever been inside?" asked Austin.

"Lor' no, Sir," answered Lubin. "Don't know as I'm over anxious to, either. The garden's a sight, it's true—but it seems there's something queer about the house. Can't make out what it can be, unless the drains are a bit out of order. But it ain't that neither. Sort o' frightening—so folks say. But lor', some folks'll say anything. I never knew anybody as ever *saw* anything there. It's only some old woman's yarn, I reckon."

"Oh, is it haunted? Are there any ghosts?" cried Austin, in great excitement. "I'd give anything in this world to see a ghost!"

"I don't know as I'd care to sleep in a haunted house myself," said Lubin, beginning to sweep the lawn. "Some folks don't mind that sort o' thing, I s'pose; must have got accustomed to it somehow. Then there's those as is born ghost-seers, and others as couldn't see one, not if it was to walk arm-in-arm with 'em to church. Let's hope Mr St Aubyn's one o' that sort, seeing as he's got to live there. It's poor work being a baker if your head's made of butter, I've heard say."

"Then it *is* haunted!" exclaimed Austin. "What a bit of luck. You see, Lubin, I know Mr St Aubyn just a little, and soon I'm going to lunch with him. How I shall be on the lookout! I wonder how it feels to see a ghost. You've never seen one, have you?"

"Oh no, Sir," replied Lubin, shaking his head. "I doubt I'm not put together that way. A blind man may shoot a crow by mistake, but he ain't no judge o' colours. Though ghosts are mostly white, they say. Well, it may be different with you, and when you go to lunch at the Court, I'm sure I hope you'll see all the ghosts on the premises if you've a fancy for that kind of wild fowl. Let ghosts leave me alone and I'll leave them alone—that's all I've got to say. I never had no hankering after gentry as go flopping around without their bodies. 'Tain't commonly decent, to my thinking.

Don't hold with such goings on myself."

"Oh, but you must make allowances for their circumstances," answered Austin. "If they've got no bodies of course they can't put them on, you know. Besides, there are ghosts and ghosts. Some are mischievous, and some are very, very unhappy, and others come to do us good and help us to find wills, and treasures, and all sorts of pleasant things. I'd love to talk with one, and have it out with him. What wonderful things one might learn!"

"Ay, there's more in the world than what's taught in the catechism," said Lubin. "Let's hope you'll have picked up a few crumbs when you've been to lunch at the Court. Every little helps, as the sow said when she swallowed the gnat. I confess I'm not curious myself."

"Well, I'm awfully curious," replied Austin, as he began to get up. "But now I must stir about a bit. You know my wooden leg gets horribly lazy sometimes, and I've got to exercise it every now and then for its own good. I know Aunt Charlotte wants me to go into the town with her to buy provender for this bun-trouble of hers tomorrow. It's very curious what different ideas of pleasure different people have."

"He's a rare sort o' boy, the young master," soliloquised Lubin as Austin went pegging along towards the house. "Game for no end of mischief when the fit takes him, for all he's only got one leg. One'd think he was half daft to hear him talk sometimes, too. Seems like as if it galled him a bit to rub along with the old auntie, and I shouldn't wonder if the old auntie herself felt about as snug as a bell-wether tied to a frisky colt. However, I s'pose the A'mighty knows what He's about, and it's always the old cow's notion as she never was a calf herself."

With which philosophical reflection Lubin slipped on his green corduroy jacket, shouldered his broom, and trudged cheerfully home to tea.

Chapter the Fourth

The next day the great heat had moderated, and the sky was covered with a thin pearly veil of gossamer greyness which afforded a delightful relief after the glare of the past week. A smart shower had fallen during the night, and the parched earth, refreshed after its bath, appeared more fragrant and more beautiful than ever. Aunt Charlotte busied herself all the morning with various household diversions, while Austin, swaying lazily to and fro in a hammock under an old apple tree, read 'Sir Gawaine and the Green Knight.' At last he looked at his watch, and found that it was about time to go and dress.

"Well, you *have* made yourself smart," commented Aunt Charlotte complacently, as Austin, sprucely attired in a pale flannel suit, with a lilac tie and a dark-red rose in his button-hole, came into the morning-room to say good-bye. "But why need you have dressed so early? Our friends aren't coming till three o'clock at the very earliest, and it's not much more than twelve—at least, so says my watch. You needn't have changed till after lunch, at any rate."

"My dear auntie, have you forgotten?" asked Austin, in innocent surprise. "Today's Thursday, and I'm engaged to lunch and spend the afternoon with Mr St Aubyn. You know I told you all about it the very day he asked me."

"Mr St Aubyn?—I don't understand," said Aunt Charlotte, with a bewildered air. "I have a recollection of your telling me a few days ago that you were lunching out some day or other, but——"

"On Thursday, you know, I said."

"Did you? Well, but—but our friends are coming *here* today! You must have been dreaming, Austin," cried Aunt Charlotte, sitting bolt upright. "How can you have made such a blunder? Of course you can't possibly go!"

"Do you really propose, auntie, that I should break my engagement with Mr St Aubyn for the sake of entertaining people like the MacTavishes and the Cobbledicks?" replied Austin, quite unmoved.

"But why did you fix on the same day?" exclaimed Aunt Charlotte desperately. "I cannot understand it. I left the date to you, you know I did—I told you I didn't care what day it was, and said you might choose whichever suited yourself best. What on earth induced you to pitch on the very day when you were invited out?"

"For the very reason you yourself assign—that you let me choose any day that suited me best. For the very reason that I *was* invited out. You see, my dear auntie——"

"Oh, you false, cunning boy!" cried Aunt Charlotte, who now saw how she had been trapped. "So you let me agree to the 24th, and took care not to tell me that the 24th was Thursday because you knew quite well I should never have consented if you had. What abominable deception! But you shall suffer for it, Austin. Of course you'll remain at home now, if only as a punishment for your deceit. I shouldn't dream of letting you go, after such disgraceful conduct. To think you could have tricked me so!"

"My dear auntie, of course I shall go," said Austin, drawing on his gloves. "Why you should wish me to stay, I cannot imagine. What on earth makes you so insistent that I should meet these friends of yours?"

"It's for your own good, you ungrateful little creature," replied Aunt Charlotte, quivering. "You know what I've always said. You require more companionship of your own age, you want to mix with other young people instead of wasting and dreaming your time away as you do, and it was for your sake, for your sake only, that I asked our friends——"

"Oh, no, auntie, it wasn't. You told me so yourself," Austin reminded her. "You told me distinctly that it was for your own pleasure and not for mine that you were going to invite them. So that argument won't do. And you were perfectly right. If you find intellectual joy in the society of Mrs Cobbledick and Shock-headed Peter——"

"Shock-headed Peter? Who in the name of fortune is that?" interrupted Aunt Charlotte, amazed.

"One of the MacTavish enchantresses—Florrie, I think, or perhaps Aggie. How am I to know? Everybody calls her Shock-headed Peter. But as I was saying, if you find happiness in the society of such people, invite them by all means. I only ask you not to cram them down my throat. I wouldn't mind the others so much, but the MacTavishes I *bar*. I will not have them forced upon me. I detest them, and I've no doubt they despise me. We simply bore each other out of our lives. There! Let that suffice. I'm very fond of *you*, auntie, and I don't want anyone else. Do you perfectly understand?"

"I shall evidently never understand *you*, Austin," replied Aunt Charlotte. "You have treated me shockingly, shockingly. And now you leave me in the most heartless way with all these people on my hands——"

"Then why did you insist on inviting them?" put in Austin. "I entreated you not to. I'd have gone down on my knees to you, only unfortunately I've only one. And when I entreated you for the last time, you said you wouldn't listen to another word. I saw that further appeal was useless, so I was compelled by you yourself to play for my own safety. So now good-bye, dear auntie. It's time I was off. Cheer up—you'll all enjoy yourselves much more without an awkward unsympathetic creature like me among you, see if you don't. And you can make any excuse for me you like," he added with a smile as he left the room. Aunt Charlotte remained transfixed.

"I suppose he must go his own gait," she muttered, as she picked up her knitting again. "There's no use in trying to force him this way or that; if he doesn't want to do a thing he won't do it. Of course what he says is true enough—I did let him choose the date, and I did ask these people because I thought it would be good for him, and I did insist on doing so when he begged me not to. Well, I'm hoist with my own petard this time, though I wouldn't confess as much to him if my life depended on it. But the trickery of the little wretch! It's that I can't get over."

Meanwhile Austin meditated on the little episode on his side, as he made his way along the road. "I daresay dear old auntie was a bit put out," he thought, "but she brought it all upon herself. She doesn't see that everybody must live his own life, that it's a duty one owes to oneself to realise one's own individuality. Now it's *bad* for me to associate with people I detest—bad for my soul's development; just as bad as it is for anyone's body to eat food that doesn't agree with him. Those MacTavishes poison my soul just as arsenic poisons the body, and I won't have my soul poisoned if I can help it. It's very sad to see how blind she is to the art and philosophy of life. But she'll have to learn it, and the sooner she begins the better."

Here he left the high road, and turned into a long, narrow lane enclosed between high banks, which led into a pleasant meadow by the river side. This shortened the way considerably, and when he reached the stile at the further end of the meadow he found himself only some ten minutes' walk from the park gates. Then a subdued excitement fell upon him. He was going to see the beautiful picture-gallery and the great collection of engravings, and the gardens with conservatories full of lovely orchids. He was going to hold delightful converse with the cultured and agreeable man to whom all these things belonged. And—well, he might possibly even see a ghost! But now, in the genial daylight, with the prospect of luncheon immediately before him, the idea of ghosts seemed rather to retire into the background. Ghosts did not appear so attractive as they had done yesterday afternoon, when he had talked about them with Lubin. However—here he was.

Mr St Aubyn, tall and middle-aged, with a refined face set in a short, pointed beard, received him with exquisite cordiality. How seldom does a man realise the positive idolatry he can inspire by treating a well-bred youth on equal terms, instead of assuming airs of patronage and condescension! The boy accepts such an attitude as natural, perhaps, but he resents it neverthe-less, and never gives the man his confidence. The perfect manners of St Aubyn won Austin's heart at once, and he responded with a modest ardour that touched and gratified his host. The Court, too, exceeded his expectations. It was a grand old mansion dating from the reign of Elizabeth, with mullioned casements, and carved doorways, and cool, dim rooms oak-panelled, and broad fireplaces; and around it lay a shining garden enclosed by old monastic walls of red brick, with shaped beds of carnations glowing redly in the sunlight, and, beyond the straight lines of lawn, a wilderness of nut-trees, with a pool of yellow waterlilies, where wild hyacinths and pale jonquils rioted when it was spring. On one side of the garden, at right angles to the house, the wall shelved into a great grass terrace, and here stood a sort of wing, flanked by two glorious old towers, crumbling and ivy-draped, forming entrances to a vast room, tapestried, which had been a banqueting hall in the picturesque Tudor days. Meanwhile, Austin was ushered by his host into the library—a moderate-sized apartment, lined with countless books and adorned with etchings of great choiceness; whence, after a few minutes' chat on indifferent subjects, they adjourned to the dining-room, where a luncheon, equally choice and good, awaited them.

At first they played a little at crosspurposes. St Aubyn, with the tact of an accomplished man entertaining a clever youth, tried to draw Austin out; while Austin, modest in the presence of one whom he recognised as infinitely his superior in everything he most valued, was far more anxious to hear St Aubyn talk than to talk himself. The result was that Austin won, and St Aubyn soon launched forth delightfully upon art, and books, and travel. He had been a great traveller in his day, and the boy listened with enraptured ears to his description of the magnificent gardens in the vicinity of Rome—the Lante, the Torlonia, the Aldobrandini, the Falconieri, and the Muti—architectural wonders that Austin had often read of, but of course had never seen; and then he talked of Viterbo and its fountains, Vicenza the city of Palladian palaces, every house a gem, and Sicily, with its hidden wonders, hidden from the track of tourists because far in the depths of the interior. He had travelled in Burma too, and inflamed the boy's imagination by telling him of the gorgeous temples of Rangoon and Mandalay; he had been—like everybody else—to Japan; and he had lived for six weeks up country in China, in a secluded Buddhist monastery perched on the edge of a precipice, like an eagle's nest, where his only associates were bonzes in yellow robes, and the stillness was only broken by the deep-toned temple bell, booming for vespers. Then, somehow, his thoughts turned back to Europe, and he began a disquisition upon the great old masters—Tintoretto, Rembrandt, Velasquez, Tiziano, and Peter Paul—with whose immortal works he seemed as familiar as he subsequently showed himself with the pictures in his own house. He described the Memlings at Bruges, the Botticellis at Florence and the Velasquezes in Spain—averring in humorous exaggeration that beside a Velasquez most other paintings were little better than chromolithographs. Austin put in a word now and then, asked a question or two as occasion served, and so suggested fresh and still more fascinating reminiscences; but he had no desire whatever to interrupt the illuminating stream of words by airing any opinions of his own. It was not until the meal was drawing to a close that the conversation took a more personal turn, and Austin was induced to say something about himself, his tastes, and his surroundings. Then St Aubyn began deftly and diplomatically to elicit something in the way of self-disclosure; and before long he was able to see exactly how things stood—the boy of ideals, of visionary and artistic tastes, of crude fresh theories and a queer philosophy of life, full of a passion for Nature and a contempt for facts, on one hand; and the excellent, commonplace, uncomprehending aunt, with her philistine friends and blundering notions as to what was good for him, upon the other. It was an amusing situation, and psychologically very interesting. St Aubyn listened attentively with a sympathetic smile as Austin stated his case.

"I see, I see," he said nodding. "You feel it imperative to lead your own life and try to live up to your own ideals. That is good—quite good. And you are not in sympathy with your aunt's friends. Nothing more natural. Of course it is important to be sure that your ideals are the highest possible. Do you think they are?"

"They seem so. They are the highest possible for *me*," replied

Austin earnestly.

"That implies a limitation," observed St Aubyn, emitting a stream of blue smoke from his lips. "Well, we all have our limitations. You appear to have a very strong sense that every man should realise his own individuality to the full; that that is his first duty to himself. Tell me then—does it never occur to you that we may also have duties to others?"

"Why, yes—certainly," said Austin. "I only mean that we have *no right* to sacrifice our own individualities to other people's ideas. For instance, my aunt, who has always been the best of friends to me, is for ever worrying me to associate with people who rasp every nerve in my body, because she thinks that it would do me good. Then I rebel. I simply will not do it."

"What friends have you?" asked St Aubyn quietly.

"I don't think I have any," said Austin, with great simplicity. "Except Lubin. My best companionship I find in books."

"The best in the world—so long as the books are good," replied St Aubyn. "But who is Lubin?"

"He's a gardener," said Austin. "About two years older than I am. But he's a gentleman, you understand. And if you could only see the sort of people my poor aunt tries to force upon me!"

"I think you may add me to Lubin—as your friend," observed St Aubyn; at which Austin flushed with pleasure. "But now, one other word. You say you want to realise your highest self. Well, the way to do it is not to live for yourself alone; it is to live for others. To save oneself one must first lose oneself—forget oneself, when occasion arises—for the sake of other people. It is only by self-sacrifice for the sake of others that the supreme heights are to be attained."

For the first time Austin's face fell. He tossed his long hair off his forehead, and toyed silently with his cigarette.

"Is that a hard saying?" resumed St Aubyn, smiling. "It has high authority, however. Think it over at your leisure. Have you finished? Come, then, and let me show you the pictures. We have the whole afternoon before us."

They explored the fine old house well-nigh from roof to basement, while St Aubyn recounted all the associations connected with the different rooms. Then they went into the picture-gallery. Austin, breathless with interest, hung upon St Aubyn's lips as he pointed out the peculiarities of each great master represented, and explained how, for instance, by a fold of the drapery or the crook of a finger, the characteristic mannerisms of the painter could be detected, and the school to which a given work belonged could approximately be determined; drew attention to the unifying and grouping of the different features of a composition; spoke learnedly of textures, qualities, and tactile values; and laid stress on the importance of colour, light, atmosphere, and the sense of motion, as contrasted with the undue preponderance too often attached by critics to mere outline. All this was new to Austin, who had really never seen any good pictures before, and his enthusiasm grew with what it fed on. St Aubyn was an admirable cicerone; he loved his pictures, and he knew them—knew everything that could be known about them—and, inspired by the intelligent appreciation of his guest, spared no pains to do them justice. A good half hour was then spent over the engravings, which were kept in a quaint old room by themselves; and afterwards they adjourned to the garden. St Aubyn's conservatories were famous, and his orchids of great variety and beauty. Austin seemed transported into a world where everything was so arranged as to gratify his craving for harmony and fitness, and he moved almost silently beside his host in a dream of satisfaction and delight.

"By the way, there's still one room you haven't seen," remarked St Aubyn, as they were strolling at their leisure through the grounds. "We call it the Banqueting Hall—in that wing between the two old towers. Queen Elizabeth was entertained there once, and it contains some rather beautiful tapestries. I should like to have them moved into the main building, only there's really no place where they'd fit, and perhaps it's better they should remain where they were originally intended for. Are you fond of tapestry?"

"I've never seen any," said Austin, "but of course I've read about it—Gobelin, Bayeux, and so on. I should love to see what it looks like in reality."

"Come, then," said St Aubyn, crossing the lawn. "I have the key in my pocket."

He flung open the door. Austin found himself in the vast apartment, groined and vaulted, measuring about a hundred and twenty feet by fifty, and lighted by exquisite pointed windows enriched with coats-of-arms and other heraldic devices in jewel-like stained glass. The walls were completely hidden by tapestries of rare beauty, woven into the semblance of gardens, palaces, arcades and bowers of clipped hedges and pleached trees with slender fountains set meetly in green shade; while some again were crowded with swaying Gothic figures of saints and kings and warriors and angels, all far too beautiful, thought Austin, to have ever lived. Yet surely there must be some prototypes of all these wonderful conceptions somewhere. There must be a world—if we could only find it—where loveliness that we only know as pictured exists in actual reality. What a dreamlike hall it was, on that still summer afternoon. Yet there was something uncanny about it too. St Aubyn had stepped out of sight, and Austin left by himself began to experience a very extraordinary sensation. He felt that he was not alone. The immense chamber seemed *full of presences*. He could see nothing, but he felt them all about him. The place was thickly populated, but the population was invisible. Everything looked as empty as it had looked when the door was first thrown open, and yet it was really full of ghostly palpitating life, crowded with the spirits of bygone men and women who had held stately revels there three hundred years before. He was not frightened, but a sense of awe crept over him, rooting him to the spot and imparting a rapt expression to his face. Did he hear anything? Wasn't there a faint rustling sound somewhere in the air behind him? No. It must have been his fancy. Everything was as silent as the grave.

He turned and saw St Aubyn close beside him. "The place is haunted!" he exclaimed in a husky voice.

"What makes you think so?" asked St Aubyn, without any intonation of surprise.

"I feel it," he replied.

"Come out," said the other abruptly. "It's curious you should say that. Other people seem to have felt the same. I'm not so sensitive myself. You're looking pale. Let's go into the library and have a cup of tea."

The hot stimulant revived him, and he was soon talking at his ease again. But the curious impression remained. It seemed to him as if he had had an experience whose effects would not be easily shaken off. He had seen no ghosts, but he had felt them, and that was quite enough. The sensation he had undergone was unmistakable; the hall was full of ghosts, and he had been conscious of their presence. This, then, was apparently what Lubin had alluded to. Oh, it was all real enough—there was no room left for any doubt whatever.

It was a quarter to five when he took leave of his entertainer, responding warmly to an injunction to look in again whenever he felt disposed. He walked very thoughtfully homewards, revolving many questions in his busy brain. How much he had seen and learnt since he left home that morning! Worlds of beauty, of art, of intellect had dawned upon his consciousness; a world of mystery too. Even now, tramping along the road, he felt a different being. Even now he imagined the presence of unseen entities—walking by his side, it might be, but anyhow close to him. Was it so? Could it be that he really was surrounded by intelligences that eluded his physical senses and yet in some mysterious fashion made their existence *known*?

At last he arrived at the stile leading into the meadow, and prepared to clamber over. Then he hesitated. Why? He could not tell. A queer, invincible repugnance to cross that stile suddenly came over him. The meadow looked fresh and green, and the road—hot, dusty, and white—was certainly not alluring; besides, he longed to saunter along the grass by the river and think over his experiences. But something prevented him. With a sense of irritation he took a few steps along the road; then the thought of the cool field reasserted itself, and with a determined effort he retraced his steps and threw one leg over the top bar of the stile. It was no use. Gently, but unmistakably, something pushed him back. He *could* not cross. He wanted to, and he was in full possession of both his physical and mental faculties, but he simply could not do it.

In great perplexity, not unmixed with some natural sense of umbrage, Austin set off again along the ugly road. The sun had come out once more, and it was very hot. What could be the matter with him? Why had he been so silly as to take the highway, with its horrid dust and glare, when the field and the lane would have been so much more pleasant? He felt puzzled and annoyed. How Mr St Aubyn would have laughed at him could he but have known. This long tramp along the disagreeable road was the only jarring incident that had befallen him that day. Well, it would soon be over. And what a day it had been, after all. How marvellous the pictures were, and the gardens; what an acquisition to his life was the friendship—not only the acquaintanceship—of St Aubyn; and then the tapestries, the great mysterious hall, and the strange revelations that had come upon him in the hall itself! At last his thoughts reverted, half in self-reproach, to Aunt Charlotte. How had she fared, meanwhile? Had she enjoyed her Cobbledicks and her MacTavishes as much as he had enjoyed his experiences at the Court?

For all his theories about living his own life and developing his own individuality, Austin was not a selfish boy. Egoistic he might be, but selfish he was not. His impulses were always generous and kindly, and he was full of thought for others. He was for ever contriving delicate little gifts for those in want, planning pleasant little surprises for people whom he loved. And now he hoped most ardently that dear Aunt Charlotte had not been very dull, and for the moment felt quite kindly towards the Cobbledicks and the MacTavishes as he reflected that, no doubt, they had helped to make his auntie happy on that afternoon.

At last he came to the entrance of the lane through which he had passed in the morning. At that moment a crowd of men and boys, most of them armed with heavy sticks and all looking terribly excited, rushed past him, and precipitated themselves into the narrow opening. He asked one of them what was the matter, but the man took no notice and ran panting after the others. So Austin pursued his way, and in a few minutes arrived at the garden gate, where to his great surprise he found Aunt Charlotte waiting for him—the picture of anxiety and terror.

"Well, auntie!—why, what's the matter?" he exclaimed, as Aunt Charlotte with a cry of relief threw herself into his arms.

"Oh, my dear boy!" she uttered in trembling agitation. "How thankful I am to see you! Which way did you come back?"

"Which way? Along the road," said Austin, much astonished. "Why?"

"Thank God!" ejaculated Aunt Charlotte. "Then you're really safe. I've been out of my mind with fear. A most dreadful thing has happened. Let us sit down a minute till I get my breath, and I'll tell you all about it."

Austin led her to a garden seat which stood near, and sat down beside her. "Well, what is it all about?" he asked.

"My dear, it was like this," began Aunt Charlotte, as she gradually recovered her composure. "Our friends were just going away—oh, I forgot to tell you that of course they came; we had a most delightful time, and dear Lottie—no, Lizzie—I always do forget which is which—I can't remember, but it doesn't matter—was the life and soul of the party; however, as I was saying, they were just going away, and I was there at the gate seeing them off, when the butcher's boy came running up and warned them on no account to venture into the road, as Hunt's dog—that's the butcher, you know—I mean Hunt is—had gone raving mad, and was loose upon the streets. Of course we were all most horribly alarmed, and wanted to know whether anybody had been bitten; but the boy was off like a shot, and two minutes afterwards the wretched dog itself came tearing past, as mad as a dog could be, its jaws a mass of foam, and snapping right and left. As soon as ever it was safe our friends took the opportunity of escaping—of course in the opposite direction; and then a crowd of villagers came along in pursuit, but not knowing which turning to take till some man or other told them that the dog had gone up the lane. Then imagine my terror! For I felt perfectly convinced that you'd be coming home that way, as the road was hot and dusty, and I know how fond you are of lanes and fields. Oh, my dear, I can't get over it even now. How was it you chose the road?"

For a moment Austin did not speak. Then he said very slowly:

"I don't know how to tell you. Of course I *could* tell you easily enough, but I don't think you'd understand. Auntie, I intended to come home by the lane. Twice or three times I tried to cross the stile into the meadows, and each time I was prevented. Something stopped me. Something pushed me back. Naturally I wanted to come by the meadow—the road was horrid—and I wanted to stroll along on the grass and enjoy myself by the river. But there it was—I couldn't do it. So I gave up trying, and came by the road after all."

"What *do* you mean, Austin?" asked Aunt Charlotte. "I never heard such a thing in my life. What was it that pushed you back?"

"I don't know," replied the boy deliberately. "I only know that something did. And as the lane is very narrow, and enclosed by excessively steep banks, the chances are that I should have met the dog in it, and that the dog would have bitten me and given me hydrophobia. And now you know as much as I do myself."

"I can't tell what to think, I'm sure," said Aunt Charlotte. "Anyhow, it's most providential that you escaped, but as for your being prevented, as you say—as for anything pushing you back—why, my dear, of course that was only your fancy. What else could it have been? I'm far too practical to believe in presentiments, and warnings, and nonsense of that sort. I'd as soon believe in table-rapping. No, my dear; I thank God you've come back safe and sound, but don't go hinting at anything supernatural, because I simply don't believe in it."

"Then why do you thank God?" asked Austin, "Isn't He supernatural? Why, He's the only really supernatural Being possible, it seems to me."

That was a poser. Aunt Charlotte, having recovered her equanimity, began to feel argumentative. It was incumbent on her to prove that she was not inconsistent in attributing Austin's preservation to the intervention of God, while disclaiming any belief in what she called the supernatural. And for the moment she did not know how to do it.

"By the supernatural, Austin," she said at last, in a very oracular tone, "I mean superstition. And I call that story of yours a piece of superstition and nothing else."

"Auntie, you do talk the most delightful nonsense of any elderly lady of my acquaintance," cried Austin, as he laughingly patted her on the back. "It's no use arguing with you, because you never can see that two and two make four. It's very sad, isn't it? However, the thing to be thankful for is that I've got back safe and sound, and that we've both had a delightful afternoon. And now tell me all your adventures. I'm dying to hear about the vicar, and the Cobbledicks, and the ingenious Jock and Sandy. Did all your friends turn up?"

"Indeed they did, and a most charming time we had," replied Aunt Charlotte briskly. "Of course they were astonished to find that you weren't here to welcome them, and I was obliged to say how unfortunate it was, but a most stupid mistake had arisen, and that you were dreadfully sorry, and all the rest of it. Ah, you don't know what you missed, Austin. The boys were full of fun as usual, and dear Lizzie—or was it Florrie? well, it doesn't matter—said she was sure you'd gone to the Court in preference because you were expecting to meet a lot of girls there who were much prettier than she was. Of course she was joking, but——"

"The vulgar, disgusting brute!" cried Austin, in sudden anger. "And these are the creatures you torment me to associate with. Well——"

"Austin, you've no right to call a young lady a brute; it's abominably rude of you," said Aunt Charlotte severely. "There was nothing vulgar in what she said; it was just a playful sally, such as any sprightly girl might indulge in. I assured her you were going to meet nobody but Mr St Aubyn himself, and then she said it was a shame that you should have been inveigled away to be bored by——"

"I don't want to hear what the woman said," interrupted Austin, with a gesture of contempt. "Such people have no right to exist. They're not worthy for a man like St Aubyn to tread upon. It's a pity you know nothing of him yourself, auntie. You wouldn't appreciate your Lotties and your Florries quite so much as you do now, if you did."

"Then you enjoyed yourself?" returned Aunt Charlotte, waiving the point. "Oh, I've no doubt he's an agreeable person in his way. And the gardens are quite pretty, I'm told. Hasn't he got a few rather nice pictures in his rooms? I'm very fond of pictures myself. Well, now, tell me all about it. How did you amuse yourself all the afternoon, and what did you talk to him about?"

But before Austin could frame a fitting answer the butcher's boy looked over the gate to tell them that the rabid dog had been found in the lane and killed.

Chapter the Fifth

It will readily be understood that Austin was in no hurry to confide anything about his experiences in the Banqueting Hall to his Aunt Charlotte. The way in which she had received his straightforward, simple account of the curious impressions which had determined his choice of a route in coming home was enough, and more than enough, to seal his tongue. He was sensitive in the extreme, and any lack of sympathy or comprehension made him retire immediately into his shell. His aunt's demeanour imparted an air of reserve even to the description he gave her of the attractions of Moorcombe Court. Perhaps the good lady was a trifle sore at never having been invited there herself. One never knows. At any rate, her attitude was chilling. So as regarded the incident in the Banqueting Hall he preserved entire silence. Her scepticism was too complacent to be attacked.

He was aroused next morning by the sweetest of country sounds—the sound of a scythe upon the lawn. Then there came the distant call of the street flowerseller, "All a-growing, all a-blowing," which he remembered as long as he could remember anything. The world was waking up, but it was yet early—not more than half past six at the very latest. So he lay quietly and contentedly in his white bed, lazily wondering how it would feel in the Banqueting Hall at that early hour, and what it would be like there in the dead of night, and how soon it would be proper for him to go and leave a card on Mr St Aubyn, and what Lubin would think of it all, and how it was he had never before noticed that great crack in the ceiling just above his head. At last he slipped carefully out of bed without waiting for Martha to bring him his hot water, and hopped as best he could to the open window and looked out. There was Lubin, mowing vigorously away, and the air was full of sweet garden scents and the early twittering of birds. He could not go back to bed after that, but proceeded forthwith to dress.

After a hurried toilet, he bumped his way downstairs; intercepted the dairyman, from whom he extorted a great draught of milk, and then went into the garden. How sweet it was, that breath of morning air! Lubin had just finished mowing the lawn, and the perfume of the cool grass, damp with the night's dew, seemed to pervade the world. No one else was stirring; there was nothing to jar his nerves; everything was harmonious, fresh, beautiful, and young. And the harmony of it all consisted in this, that Austin was fresh, and beautiful, and young himself.

"Well, and how did ye fare at the Court?" asked Lubin, as Austin joined him. "Was it as fine a place as you reckoned it would be?"

"Oh, Lubin, it was lovely!" cried Austin, enthusiastically. "I do wish you could see it. And the garden! Of course this one's lovely too, and I love it, but the garden at the Court is simply divine. It's on a great scale, you know, and there are huge orchid-houses, and flaming carnations, and stained tulips, and gilded lilies, and a wonderful grass terrace, and—"

"Ay, ay, I've heard tell of all that," interrupted Lubin. "But how about the ghosts? Did you see any o' them, as you was so anxious about?"

"No—I didn't see any; but they're there all the same," returned Austin. "I felt them, you know. But only in one place; that great room, they say, was a Banqueting Hall once upon a time. You know, Lubin, I'm going back there before long. Mr St Aubyn asked me to come again, and I intend to go into that room again to see if I feel anything more. It was the very queerest thing! I never felt so strange in my life. The place seemed actually full of them. I could feel them all round me, though I couldn't see a thing. And the strangest part of it is that I've never felt quite the same since."

"How d'ye mean?" asked Lubin, looking up.

"I don't know—but I fancy I may still be surrounded by them in some sort of way," replied Austin. "It's possibly nothing but imagination after all. However, we shall see. Now this morning I want to go a long ramp into the country—as far as the Beacon, if I can. It's going to be a splendid day, I'm sure."

"I'm not," said Lubin. "The old goose was dancing for rain on the green last night, and that's a sure sign of a change."

"Dancing for rain! What old goose?" asked Austin, astonished.

"The geese always dance when they want rain," replied Lubin, "and what the goose asks for God sends. Did you never hear that before? It's a sure fact, that is. It'll rain within four-and-twenty hours, you mark my words."

"I hope it won't," said Austin. "And so your mother keeps geese?"

"Ay, that she does, and breeds 'em, and fattens 'em up against Michaelmas. And we've a fine noise o' ducks on the pond, too. They pays their way too, I reckon."

"A noise o' ducks? What, do they quack so loud?"

"Lor' bless you, Master Austin, where was you brought up? Everybody hereabouts know what a noise o' ducks is. Same as a flock o' geese, only one quacks and the other cackles. Well, now I'm off home, for its peckish work mowing on an empty belly, and the mother'll be looking out for me. Geese for me, ghosts for you, and in the end we'll see which pans out the best."

So Lubin trudged away to his breakfast and left Austin to his reflections. The predicted rain held off in spite of the terpsichorean importunity of Lubin's geese, and Austin passed a lovely morning on the moors; but next day it came down with a vengeance, and for six hours there was a regular deluge. However, Austin didn't mind. When it was fine he spent his days in the fields and woods; if it rained, he sat at a window where he could watch the grey mists, and the driving clouds, and the straight arrows of water falling wonderfully through the air. His books, too, were a resource that never failed, and if he was unable personally to participate in beautiful scenes, he could always read about them, which was the next best thing after all.

The weather continued unsettled for some days, and then it cleared up gloriously, so that Austin was able to lead what he called his Daphnis life once more. The rains had had rather a depressing effect upon his general health, and once or twice he had fancied that something was troubling him in his stump; but with the return of the sun all such symptoms disappeared as though by magic, and he felt younger and lighter than ever as he stepped forth again into the glittering air. More than a week had elapsed since his day at the Court, and he began to think that now he really might venture to go and call. So off he set one sunny afternoon, and with rather a beating heart presented himself at the park gates.

Here, however, a disappointment awaited him. The lodge-keeper shook his head, and announced that Mr St Aubyn was away and wouldn't be back till night. Austin could do nothing but leave a card, and hope that he might be lucky enough to meet him by accident before long.

So he turned back and made for the meadow by the river side, feeling sure that he would be safe from rabid dogs that time at any rate. And certainly no mysterious influences intervened to prevent him sitting on the stile for a rest, and indulging in pleasant thoughts. Then he pulled out his pocket-volume of the beloved Eclogues, and read the musical contest between Menalcas and Damætas with great enjoyment. Why, he wondered, were there no delightful shepherd-boys nowadays, who spent their time in lying under trees and singing one against the other? Lubin was much nicer than most country lads, but even Lubin was not equal to improvising songs about Phyllis, and Delia, and the Muses. Then he looked up, and saw a stranger approaching him across the field.

He was a big, stoutish man, with a fat face, a frock-coat tightly buttoned up, a large umbrella, and a rather shabby hat of the shape called chimney-pot. A somewhat incongruous object, amid that rural scene, and not a very prepossessing one; but apparently a gentleman, though scarcely of the stamp of St Aubyn. At last he came quite near, and Austin moved as though to let him pass.

"Don't trouble yourself, young gentleman," said the newcomer, in a good-humoured, offhand way. "Can you tell me whether I'm anywhere near a place called Moorcombe Court?"

"Yes—it's not far off," replied Austin, immediately interested. "I've just come from there myself."

"Really, now!" was the gentleman's rejoinder. "And how's me friend St Aubyn?"

So he was Mr St Aubyn's friend—or claimed to be. "I really suspected," said Austin to himself, "that he must be a bailiff." From which it may be inferred that the youth's acquaintance with bailiffs was somewhat limited. Then he said, aloud:

"I believe he's quite well, thank you, but I'm afraid you'll not be able to see him. He's gone out somewhere for the day."

"Dear me, now, that's a pity!" exclaimed the stranger, taking off his hat and wiping his hot, bald head. "Dear old Roger—it's years since we met, and I was quite looking forward to enjoying a chat with him about old times. Well, well, another day will do, no doubt. You don't live at the Court, do you?"

"I? Oh, no," said Austin. "I only visit there. It is such a charming place!"

"Shouldn't wonder," remarked the other, nodding. "Our friend's a rich man, and can afford to gratify his tastes—which are rather expensive ones, or used to be when I knew him years ago. I must squeeze an hour to go and see him some time or other while I'm here, if I can only manage it."

"Then you are not here for long?" asked Austin, wondering who the man could be.

"Depends upon business, young gentleman," replied the stranger. "Depends upon how we draw. We shall have a week for certain, but after that——"

"How you draw?" repeated Austin, politely mystified.

"Yes, draw—what houses we draw, to be sure," explained the stranger. "What, haven't you seen the bills? I'm on tour with 'Sardanapalus'!"

A ray of light flashed upon Austin's memory. "Oh! I think I understand," he ventured hesitatingly. "Are you—can you perhaps be—er—Mr Buckskin?"

"For Buckskin read Buskin, and you may boast of having hazarded a particularly shrewd guess," replied the gentleman. "Bucephalus Buskin, at your service; and, of course, the public's."

"Ah, now I know," exclaimed Austin. "The greatest actor in Europe, on or off the stage."

"Oh come, now, come; spare my blushes, young gentleman, draw it a *little* milder!" cried the delighted manager, almost bursting with mock modesty. "Greatest actor in Europe—oh, very funny, very good indeed! Off the stage, too! Oh dear, dear, dear, what wags there are in the world! And pray, young gentleman, from whom did you pick up that?"

"I think it must have been the milkman," replied Austin simply.

"The milkman, eh? A most discriminating milkman, 'pon my word. Well, it's always encouraging to find appreciation of high art, even among milkmen," observed Mr Buskin. "Only shows how much we owe the growing education of the masses to the drama. Talk of the press, the pulpit, the schoolroom——"

"I believe he was quoting an advertisement," interpolated Austin.

"An ad., eh?" said the mummer, somewhat disconcerted. "Oh, well, I shouldn't be surprised. Of course *I* have nothing to do with such things. That's the business of the advance-agent. And did he really put in that? I positively must speak to him about it. A good fellow, you know, but rather inclined to let his zeal outrun his discretion. It's not good business to raise too great expectations, is it, now?"

Austin, in his innocence, scarcely took in the meaning of all this. But it was clear enough that Mr Buskin was a great personage in his way, and extremely modest into the bargain. His interest was now very much excited, and he awaited eagerly what the communicative gentleman would say next.

"I should think it would take," continued Mr Buskin, warming to his subject. "It's a most magnificent spectacle when it's properly done—as we do it. There's a scene in the third act—the Banquet in the Royal Palace—that's something you won't forget as long as you live. A gorgeous hall, brilliantly illuminated—the whole Court in glittering costumes—the tables covered with gold and silver plate. Peals of thunder, and a frightful tempest raging outside. In the midst of the revels a conspiracy breaks out—enter Pania, bloody—Sardanapalus assumes a suit of armour, and admires himself in a looking-glass—and then the rival armies burst in, and a terrific battle ensues——"

"What, in the dining-room?" asked the astonished Austin.

"Well, well, the poet allows himself a bit of licence there, I admit; but that only gives us an opportunity of showing what fine stage-management can do," said Mr Buskin complacently. "It's a magnificent situation. You'll say you never saw anything like it since you were born, you just mark my words."

"It certainly must be very wonderful," remarked Austin. "But I'm afraid I'm rather ignorant of such matters. What *is* 'Sardanapalus,' may I ask?"

"What, never heard of Byron's 'Sardanapalus'?" exclaimed the actor, throwing up his hands. "Why, it's one of the finest things ever put upon the boards. Full of telling effects, and not too many bothering lengths, you know. The Poet Laureate, dear good man, worried my life out a year ago to let him write a play upon the subject especially for me. The part of Sardanapalus was to be devised so as to bring out all my particular—er—capabilities, and any little hints that might occur to me were to be acted upon and embodied in the text. But I wouldn't hear of it. 'Me dear Alfred,' I said, 'it isn't that I underrate your very well-known talents, but Byron's good enough for *me*. Hang it all, you know, an artist owes something to the classics of his country.' So now, if that uneasy spirit ever looks this way from the land of the eternal shades, he'll see something at least to comfort him. He'll see that one actor, at least, not unknown to Europe, has vindicated his reputation as a playwright in the face of the British public."

Austin felt immensely flattered at such confidences being vouchsafed to him by the eminent exponent of Lord Byron, and said he was certain that the theatre would be crammed. Mr Buskin shrugged his shoulders, and replied he was sure he hoped so.

"And now," he added, "I think I'll be walking back. And look you here, young gentleman. We've had a pleasant meeting, and I'd like to see you again. Just take this card"—scribbling a few words on it in pencil—"and the night you favour us with your presence in the house, come round and see me in me dressing-room between the acts. You've only to show that, and they'll let you in at once. I'd like your impressions of the thing while it's going on."

Austin accepted the card with becoming courtesy, and offered his own in exchange. Mr Buskin shook hands in a very cordial manner, and the next moment was making his way rapidly in the direction of the town.

"What a very singular gentleman," thought Austin, when he was once more alone. "I wonder whether all actors are like that. Scarcely, I suppose. Well, now I'm to have a glimpse of another new world. Mr St Aubyn has shown me one or two; what will Mr Buskin's be like? It's all extremely interesting, anyhow."

Then he stumped along to the river side, giving a majestic twirl to his wooden leg with every step he took through the long grass. How he would have loved a bathe! The pool where he had so enjoyed himself with Lubin was not far off—the pool of Daphnis, as he had christened it; but he hesitated to venture in alone. So he lay down on the bank and watched the yellow waterlilies from afar, dreaming of many things. How clever Lubin was, and what a lot he knew! Why geese should dance for rain he couldn't even imagine; but the rain had actually come, and it was all a most suggestive mystery. How many other curious connections there must be among natural occurrences that nobody ever dreamt of! It was in the country one learnt about such things; in the fields and woods, and by the side of rivers. Nature was the great school, after all. History and geography were all very well in their way, but what food for the soul was there in knowing whether Norway was an island or a peninsula, or on what date some silly king had had his crown put on? What did it matter, after all? Those were the facts he despised; facts that had no significance for him whatever, that left him exactly as they found him first. The sky and the birds and the flowers taught him lessons that were worth more than all the histories and geographies that were ever written. The schoolroom was a desert, arid and unsatisfying; whereas the garden, the enclosed space which held stained cups of beauty and purple gold-eyed bells, that was a jewelled sanctuary. Lubin was nearer the heart of things than Freeman and Macaulay, though they would have disdained him as a clod. Virgil and Theocritus were greater philosophers than either Comte or Hegel. Daphnis and Corydon represented the finest flower, the purest type of human evolution, and Herbert Spencer was nothing better than a particularly silly old man.

Having disposed of the education question thus conclusively, it occurred to Austin that it must be about time for tea; so he struggled to his legs and turned his footsteps homeward. Just as he arrived at the house he met Lubin outside the gate with a wheelbarrow.

"Off already?" he asked.

"Ay," said Lubin. "I say, Master Austin, there's something I want to tell you. I see a magpie not an hour ago!"

"A magpie? I don't think I ever saw one in my life. What was it like?" enquired Austin.

"Don't matter what it was like," replied Lubin, sententiously. "But it was just outside your bedroom window. You'd better be on the lookout."

"What for?" asked Austin. "Did it say it was coming back?"

"'Tain't nothing to laugh at," said Lubin, nodding his head. "A magpie bodes ill-luck. That's well known, that is. So you just keep your eye open, that's all I've got to say. It's a warning, you see. Did ye never hear that before?"

Austin's first impulse was to laugh; then he remembered the dancing goose, and the rain which followed in due course. "All right, Lubin," he said cheerfully. "I'm not afraid of magpies; I don't think they're very dangerous. But I *have* heard that they've a fancy for silver spoons, so I'll tell Aunt Charlotte to lock the plate up safely before she goes to bed."

As he had expected, Aunt Charlotte was much pleased at hearing of his encounter with Mr Buskin, who, she thought, must be a most delightful person. It would be so good, too, for Austin to see something of the gay world instead of always mooning about alone; and then he would be sure to meet other young people at the performance, friends from the neighbouring town, with whom he could talk and be sociable. Austin, on his side, was quite willing to go and be amused, though he felt, perhaps, more interested in what promised to be an entirely new experience than excited at the prospect of a treat. He wanted to see and to study, and then he would be able to judge.

"By the way, Austin," said his aunt, as they were separating for the night a few hours later, "I want you to go into the town tomorrow and tell Snewin to send a man up at once to look at the roof. I'm afraid it's been in rather a bad state for some time past, and those heavy rains we had last week seem to have damaged it still more. Be sure you don't forget. It won't do to have a leaky roof over our heads; it might come tumbling down, and cost a mint of money to put right again."

Austin gave the required promise, and thought no more about it. He also forgot entirely to tell his aunt she had better lock up the spoons with particular care that night because Lubin had seen a magpie in suspicious proximity to his window. He went straight up to his room, feeling rather sleepy, and bent on getting between the sheets as soon as possible. But just as he was putting on his nightgown, a light pattering sound attracted his attention, and he immediately became all ears.

"Rain?" he exclaimed. "Why, there wasn't a sign of it an hour ago!"

He drew up the blind and looked out. The sky was perfectly clear, and a brilliant moon was shining.

"That's queer!" he murmured. "I could have sworn I heard it raining. What in the world could it have been?"

He turned away and put out the candle. As he approached the bed a curious disinclination to get into it came over him. Then he heard the same pattering noise again. He stopped short, and listened more attentively. It seemed to come from the walls.

A shower of raps, rather like tiny explosions, now sounded all around him. He leant his head against the wall, and the sound became distincter. This time there was no mistake about it. He had never heard anything like it in his life. He was quite cool, not in the least frightened, and very much on the alert. The raps continued at intervals for about five minutes. Then, seeing that it was impossible to solve the mystery, he suddenly jumped into bed. At that moment the raps ceased.

For nearly an hour he lay awake, wondering. Certainly he had not been the victim of hallucination. He was in perfect health, and in full possession of all his faculties. Indeed his faculties were particularly alive; he had been thinking of something else altogether when the raps first forced themselves upon his consciousness, and afterwards he had listened to them for several minutes with close and critical attention. No explanation of the strange phenomenon suggested itself in spite of endless theories and speculations. Could it be mice? But mice only gnawed and scuttled about; they did not rap. It was more like crackling than anything else; the noise produced by thousands of faint discharges. No, it was inexplicable, and he wondered more and more.

Gradually he fell asleep. How long he slept he didn't know, but he awoke with a sensation of cold. Instinctively he put out his hand to pull the coverings closer over him, and found that they seemed to have slipped down somehow, leaving his chest exposed. Then, warm again, he dozed off once more and dreamt that he was at the pool of Daphnis with Lubin. How cool and blue the water looked, and how lovely the plunge would be! But when he was stripped the weather suddenly changed; a chill wind sprang up which made his teeth chatter; and then Lubin—who somehow wasn't Lubin but had unaccountably turned into Mr Buskin—insisted on throwing him into the water, which now looked cold and black. He struggled furiously, and awoke shivering.

There was not a rag upon him. Again he stretched out his hand to feel for the clothes, but they had disappeared. Instinctively he threw himself out of bed and flung open the shutters. The moon had set, and the first faint gleams of approaching dawn filtered into the room, showing, to his amazement, the bedclothes drawn completely away from the mattress and hanging over the rail at the foot, so as to be quite out of the reach of his hand as he had lain there. What on earth was the matter with the bed? Was it bewitched? Who had uncovered him in that unceremonious way, leaving him perished with cold? No wonder he had dreamt of that chilly wind, numbing his body as he stood naked by the pool. Had he by any chance kicked the coverlet off in his sleep, as he engaged in that dream-struggle with the absurdly impossible Buskin-Lubin who had attempted to pitch him into the dark water? Clearly not; for that would not account for the sheet and blanket being dragged so carefully out of the range of his hands, and hung over the footrail so that they touched the floor.

Such were the thoughts that flashed through his mind as he stood motionless by the window, with wide open eyes, in the chill morning light. Suddenly a rending, bursting noise was heard in the ceiling. The crack widened into a chasm, and then, with a heavy thud, down fell a confused mass of old bricks, crumbling mortar, and rotten, wormeaten wood full on the mattress he had just relinquished, scattering pulverised rubble in all directions, and covering the bed with a layer of horrible dust and *débris*.

Chapter the Sixth

Had her very life depended on it, old Martha would have been totally unable to give any coherent account of what she felt, said, or did, when she came into Master Austin's room that morning at half past seven with his hot water. She thought she must have screamed, but such was her bewilderment and terror she really could not remember whether she did or no. But she never had any doubt as to what she saw. Instead of a fair white bed with Austin lying in it, she was confronted by the sight of a gaping hole in the roof, something that looked like a rubbish heap in a brickfield immediately underneath, and the long slender form of Austin himself wrapped in a comfortable wadded dressing-gown fast asleep upon the sofa. "Bless us and save us!" she ejaculated under her breath. "And to think that the boy's lived through it!"

Austin, roused by her entrance, yawned, stretched himself, and lazily opened his eyes. "Is that you already, Martha?" he said. "Oh, how sleepy I am. Is it really half past seven?"

"But what does it all mean—how it is you're not killed?" cried Martha, putting down the jug, and finding her voice at last. "The good Lord preserve us—here's the house tumbling down about our ears and never a one of us the wiser. And the man was to 'ave come this very day to see to that blessed roof. Come, wake up, do, Master Austin, and tell me how it happened."

"Is Aunt Charlotte up yet?" asked Austin turning over on his side.

"Ay, that she be, and making it lively for the maids downstairs. Whatever will she say when she hears about this to-do?" exclaimed Martha, with her hands upon her hips as she gazed at the desolation round her.

"Well, please go down and ask her to come up here at once," said Austin. "I see I shall have to say something, and it really will be too much bother to go over it to everybody in turn. I've had rather a disturbed night, and feel most awfully tired. So just run down and bring her up as soon as ever you can, and then we'll get it over."

"A pretty business—and me with forty-eleven things to do already today," muttered the old servant as she hurried out. "True it is that except the Lord builds the house they labour in vain as builds it. He didn't have no hand in building this one, that's as plain as I am—as never was a beauty at my best. Well, the child's safe, that's one mercy. Though what he was doing out of his bed when the roof came down's a mystery to *me*. Talking to the moon, I shouldn't wonder. The good Lord's got 'is own ways o' doing things, and it ain't for the likes of us to pick holes when they turn out better than the worst."

Meanwhile Austin lay quietly and drowsily on his couch piecing things together. Seen from the distance of a few hours, now that he had leisure to reflect, how wonderfully they fitted in! First of all, there had been that sudden outburst of raps just as he was stepping into bed. That, evidently, was intended as a warning. It was as much as to say, "Don't! don't!" But of course he couldn't be expected to know this, and so he could only wonder where the raps came from, and get into bed as usual. Then, the instant he did so the raps ceased. That was because it wasn't any use to go on. The rappers, he supposed, had benevolently tried to frighten him away, and induce him to go and sleep on the sofa at the other end of the room where he was now; but the attempt had failed. So there was nothing for them to do, as he was actually in bed, but to get him out again; and this they had succeeded in doing by dragging all his clothes off. Now he saw it all. Nothing, it seemed to him, could possibly be clearer. But who were the unseen friends who had thus interposed to save his life? Ah, that was a secret still.

Then footsteps were heard outside, and in bustled Aunt Charlotte, with Martha chattering in her wake. Austin raised himself upon his cushions, and then sank back again. "Lord save us!" cried Aunt Charlotte, coming to a dead stop, as she surveyed the ruins.

"It's rather a mess, isn't it?" remarked Austin, folding a red table-cover round his single leg by way of counterpane.

"A mess!" repeated Aunt Charlotte. "I should think it *was* a mess. How in the world, Austin, did you manage to escape?"

"Well—I happened to get out of bed a minute or two before the ceiling broke," said Austin, "and it's just as well I did. Otherwise my artless countenance would have got rather disfigured, and I might even have been hurt. You see all that raw material isn't composed of gossamer——"

"What time did it occur?" asked Aunt Charlotte, shortly.

"The dawn was just breaking. I suppose it must have been about four o'clock, but I didn't look at my watch," replied Austin. "I was too cold and sleepy."

"Cold and sleepy!" exclaimed Aunt Charlotte. "And the house collapsing over your head. You seem to have had time to pull the bedclothes away, though. That's very curious. What did you do that for?"

"I didn't," replied Austin.

"Then who did?" asked Aunt Charlotte, getting more and more excited. "I do wish you'd be a little more communicative, Austin; I have to drag every word out of you as though you were trying to hide something. Who hung the bedclothes over the footrail if you didn't?"

"I can't tell you. I don't know. All I know is that I found them where they are now when I woke up, and I woke up because I was so cold. Then I got out of bed, and a minute afterwards down came all the bricks."

"Do you mean to tell me——" began Aunt Charlotte, in her most scathing tones.

"Certainly I do. Exactly what I *have* told you. Why?"

"Do you expect me to believe," resumed his aunt, "that somebody came into the room when you were asleep, and deliberately pulled off all your bedclothes for the fun of doing it? Am I to understand——"

"My dear auntie, I am not an idiot, nor am I in the habit of perjuring myself," interrupted Austin. "I saw nobody come into the room, and I saw nobody pull off the clothes. If you really want to know what I 'expect you to believe,' I've already told you. I might tell you a little more, but then I shouldn't expect you to believe it, so what would be the good? It seems to me the best thing to do now is to send for Snewin to take away all this mess, move the furniture, and mend the hole in the ceiling. If once it begins to rain——"

"Oh! You might tell me a little more, might you?" said Aunt Charlotte, bristling. "So you haven't told me everything after all. Now, then, never mind whether I believe it or not, that's my affair. What is there more to tell?"

"Nothing," replied Austin. "Because it isn't only your affair whether you believe me or not; it's my affair as well. Why, you don't even believe what I've told you already! So I won't tax your credulity any further."

Aunt Charlotte now began to get rather angry, "Look here, Austin," she said, "I intend to get to the bottom of this business, so it's not the slightest use trying to beat about the bush. I insist on your telling me how it was you happened to get out of bed just before the accident occurred, and how the bedclothes came to be pulled away and hung where they are now. There's a mystery about the whole thing, and I hate mysteries, so you'd better make a clean breast of it at once."

"Had I?" said Austin, pretending to reflect. "I wonder whether it would be wise. You see, dear auntie, you're such a sensitive creature; your nerves are so highly strung, you're so easily frightened out of your dear old wits—"

"Be done with all this nonsense!" snapped Aunt Charlotte brusquely. "Come, I can't stand here all day. Just tell me exactly what took place—why you woke up, and what you saw, and everything about it you remember."

"Dear auntie, I don't want you to stand there all day; in fact I'd much rather you didn't stand there a minute longer, because I want to get up," Austin assured her earnestly. "I awoke because I had a horrid dream, caused by the cold which in its turn was produced by my being left with nothing on. And I didn't see anything, for the simple reason that the room was as dark as pitch. Is there anything else you want to know?"

"Yes, there is. Everything that you haven't told me," said the uncompromising aunt.

"Very well, then," said Austin, leaning upon his elbow and looking her full in the face. "But on one condition only—that you believe every word I say."

"Of course, Austin, I should never dream of doubting your good faith," replied Aunt Charlotte. "But don't romance. Now then."

"It's very simple, after all," began Austin. "Just as I was getting into bed a strange noise, like a shower of little raps, broke out all around me. It went on for nearly five minutes, and I was listening all the time and trying to find out what it was and where it came from. At the moment I had no clue, but now I fancy I can guess. Those raps were warnings. They—the rappers—were trying to prevent me getting into bed. They didn't succeed, of course, and so, just as the ceiling was on the point of giving way, they compelled me to get out of bed by pulling all the clothes off. If they hadn't, I should have been half killed. Now, what do you make of that?"

"I knew it must be some nonsense of the sort!" exclaimed Aunt Charlotte, in her most vigorous tones. "Raps, indeed! I never heard such twaddle. Of course I don't doubt your word, but it's clear enough that you dreamt the whole thing. You always were a dreamer, Austin, and you're getting worse than ever. I don't believe you know half the time whether you're asleep or awake."

"Did I dream *that*?" asked Austin, pointing to the bedclothes as they hung.

"You dragged them there in your sleep, of course," retorted Aunt Charlotte triumphantly. "I see the whole thing now. You had a dream, you kicked the clothes off in your sleep, and then you got out of bed, still in your sleep——"

"I didn't do anything of the sort," interrupted Austin. "I was wide awake the whole time. You see, auntie, I was here and you weren't, so I ought to know something about it."

"It's no use arguing with you," replied Aunt Charlotte, loftily. "It's a clear case of sleepwalking—as clear as any case I ever heard of. And then all that nonsense about raps! Of course, if you heard anything at all—which I only half believe—it was something beginning to give way in the roof. There! It only requires a little common-sense, you see, to explain the whole affair. And now, my dear——"

"Hush!" whispered Austin suddenly.

"What's the matter?" exclaimed Aunt Charlotte, not liking to be interrupted.

"Listen!" said Austin, under his breath.

A torrent of raps burst out in the wall immediately behind him, plainly audible in the silence. Then they stopped, as suddenly as they had begun.

"Did you hear them?" said Austin. "Those were the raps I told you of. Hark! There they are again. I wish they would sound a little louder." A distinct increase in the sound was noticeable. "Oh, isn't it perfectly wonderful? Now, what have you to say?"

Aunt Charlotte stood agape. It was no use pretending she didn't hear them. They were as unmistakable as knocks at a front door.

"What jugglery is this?" she demanded, in an angry tone.

"Really, dear auntie, I am not a conjurer," replied Austin, as he sank back upon his cushions. "That was what I heard last night. But of course *you* don't believe in such absurdities. It's only your fancy after all, you know."

"'Tain't *my* fancy, anyhow," put in old Martha, speaking for the first time. "I heard 'em plain enough. 'Tis the 'good people,' for sure."

"Hold your tongue, do!" cried Aunt Charlotte in sore perplexity. "Good people, indeed!—the devil himself, more likely. I tell you what it is, Austin——"

"Why, I thought you weren't superstitious!" observed Austin, in a tone of most exasperating surprise. Three gentle knocks, running off into a ripple of pattering explosions, were then heard in a farther corner of the room. "There, don't you hear them laughing at you? Thank you, dear people, whoever you are, that was very kind. And it was awfully sweet of you to save me from those bricks last night. It *was* good of them, wasn't it, auntie dear?"

"If all this devilry goes on I shall take serious measures to stop it," gasped Aunt Charlotte, who was almost frightened to death. "I cannot and will not live in a haunted house. It's you who are haunted, Austin, and I shall go and see the vicar about it this very day. It's an awful state of things, positively awful. To think that you are actually holding communication with familiar spirits! The vicar shall come here at once, and I'll get him to hold a service of exorcism. I believe there is such a service, and——"

"Oh, do, do, *do!*" screamed Austin, clapping his hands with delight. "What fun it would be! Fancy dear Mr Sheepshanks, in all his tippets and toggery, ambling and capering round poor me, and trying to drive the devil out of me with a broomful of holy water! That's a lovely idea of yours, auntie. Lubin shall come and be an acolyte, and we'll get Mr Buskin to be stage-manager, and you shall be the pew-opener. And then I'll empty the holy-water pot over dear Mr Sheepshanks' head when he's looking the other way. You *are* a genius, auntie, though you're too modest to be conscious of it. But you're very ungrateful all the same, for if it hadn't been for——"

"There, stop your ribaldry, Austin, and get up," said Aunt Charlotte, impatiently. "The sooner we're all out of this dreadful room the better. And let me tell you that you'd be better employed in thanking God for your deliverance than in turning sacred subjects into ridicule."

"Thanking God? Why, not a moment ago you said it was the devil!" exclaimed Austin. "How you do chop and change about, auntie. You can't possibly expect me to be orthodox when you go on contradicting yourself at such a rate. However, if you really must go, I think I *will* get up. It must be long past eight, and I want my breakfast awfully."

The day so excitingly ushered in turned out a busy one. As soon as he had finished his meal, Austin pounded off to invoke the immediate presence of Mr Snewin the builder, and before long there was a mighty bustle in the house. The furniture had all to be removed from the scene of the disaster, the bed cleared of the *débris*, preparations made for the erection of light scaffolding for repairing the roof, and Austin himself installed, with all his books and treasures, in another bedroom overlooking a different part of the garden. It was all a most enjoyable adventure, and even Aunt Charlotte forgot her terrors in the more practical necessities of the occasion. Just before lunch Austin snatched a few minutes to run out and gossip with Lubin on the lawn. Lubin listened with keen interest to the boy's picturesque account of his experiences, and then remarked, sagely nodding his head:

"I told you to be on the lookout, you know, Master Austin. Magpies don't perch on folks' windowsills for nothing. You'll believe me a little quicker next time, maybe."

For once in his life Austin could think of nothing to say in reply. To ask Lubin to explain the connection between magpies and misadventures would have been useless; it evidently sufficed for him that such was the order of Nature, and only a magpie would have been able to clear up the mystery. Besides, there are many such mysteries in the world. Why do cats occasionally wash their heads behind the ear? Clearly, to tell us that we may expect bad weather; for the bad weather invariably follows. These are all providential arrangements intended for our personal convenience, and are not to be accounted for on any cut-and-dried scientific theory. Lubin's erudition was certainly very great, but there was something exasperating about it too.

So Austin went in to lunch thoughtful and dispirited, wondering why there were so many absurdities in life that he could neither elucidate nor controvert. He decided not to say anything to Aunt Charlotte about Lubin's magpie sciolisms, lest he should provoke a further outburst of the discussion they had held in the morning; he had had the best of that, anyhow, and did not care to compromise his victory by dragging in extraneous considerations in which he did not feel sure of his ground. Aunt Charlotte, on her side, was inclined to be talkative, taking refuge in the excitement of having workmen in the house from the uneasy feelings which still oppressed her in consequence of those frightening raps. But now that the haunted room was to be invaded by friendly, commonplace artisans from the village, and turned inside out, and almost pulled to pieces, there was a chance that the ghosts would be got rid of without invoking the aid of Mr Sheepshanks; a reflection that inspired her with hope, and comforted her greatly.

"You know you're a great anxiety to me, Austin," she said, as, refreshed by food and wine, she took up her knitting after lunch. "I wish you were more like other boys, indeed I do. I never could understand you, and I suppose I never shall."

"But what does that matter, auntie?" asked Austin. "I don't understand *you* sometimes, but that doesn't make me anxious in the very least. Why you should worry yourself about me I can't conceive. What do I do to make you anxious? I don't get tipsy, I don't gamble away vast fortunes at a sitting, and although I'm getting on for eighteen I haven't had a single action for breach of promise brought against me by anybody. Now *I* think that's rather a creditable record. It isn't everybody who can say as much."

"I want you to be more *serious*, Austin," replied his aunt, "and not to talk such nonsense as you're talking now. I want you to be sensible, practical, and alive to the sober facts of life. You're too dreamy a great deal. Soon you won't know the difference between dreams and realities——"

"I don't even now. No more do you. No more does anybody," interrupted Austin, lighting a cigarette.

"There you are again!" exclaimed Aunt Charlotte, clicking her needles energetically. "Did one ever hear such rubbish? It all comes from those outlandish books you're always poring over. If you'd only take *my* advice, you'd read something solid, and sensible, and improving, like 'Self Help,' by Dr Smiles. That would be of some use to you, but these others——"

"I read a whole chapter of it once," said Austin. "I can scarcely believe it myself, but I did. It's the most immoral, sordid, selfish book that was ever printed. It deifies Success—success in money-making—success of the coarsest and most materialistic kind. It is absolutely unspiritual and degrading. It nearly made me sick."

"Be silent!" cried Aunt Charlotte, horrified. "How dare you talk like that? I will not sit still and hear you say such things. Few books have had a greater influence upon the age. Degrading? Why, it's been the making of thousands!"

"Thousands of soulless money-grubbers," retorted Austin. "That's what it has made. Men without an idea or an aspiration above their horrible spinning-jennies and account-books. I hate your successful stockbrokers and shipowners and manufacturers. They are an odious race. Wasn't it a stockjobber who thought Botticelli was a cheese? Everyone knows the story, and I believe the hero of it was either a stockjobber or a man who made screws in Birmingham."

Aunt Charlotte let her knitting fall on her lap in despair. "Austin," she said, in her most solemn tones, "I never regretted your poor mother's death as I regret it at this moment."

"Why, auntie?" he asked, surprised.

"Perhaps she would have understood you better; perhaps she might even have been able to manage you," replied the poor lady. "I confess that you're beyond me altogether. Do you know what it was she said to me upon her deathbed? 'Charlotte,' she said, 'my only sorrow in dying is that I shall never be able to bring up my boy. Who will ever take such care of him as I should?' You were then two days old, and the very next day she died. I've never forgotten it. She passed away with that sorrow, that terrible anxiety, tearing at her heart. I took her place, as you know, but of course I was only a makeshift. I often wonder whether she is still as anxious about you as she was then."

"My dearest auntie, you've been an angel in a lace cap to me all my life, and I'm sure my mother isn't worrying herself about me one bit. Why should she?" argued Austin. "I'm leading a lovely life, I'm as happy as the days are long, and if my tastes don't run in the direction of selling screws or posting ledgers, nothing that anybody can say will change them. And I tell you candidly that if they were so changed they would certainly be changed for the worse. I hate ugly things as intensely as I love beautiful ones, and I'm very thankful that I'm not ugly myself. Now don't look at me like that; it's so conventional! Of course I know I'm not ugly, but rather the reverse (that's a modest way of putting it), and I pray to beloved Pan that he will give me beauty in the inward soul so that the inward and the outward man may be at one. That's out of the 'Phædrus,' you know—a very much superior composition to 'Self Help.' So cheer up, auntie, and don't look on me as a doomed soul because we're not both turned out of the same meltingpot. Now I'm just going upstairs to see to the arrangement of my new room, and then I shall go and help Lubin in the garden."

So saying, he strolled out. But poor Aunt Charlotte only shook her head. She could not forget how Austin's mother had grieved at not living to bring up her boy, and wished more earnestly than ever that the responsibility had fallen into other hands than hers. There was something so dreadfully uncanny about Austin. His ignorance about the common facts of life was as extraordinary as his perfect familiarity with matters known only to great scholars. His views and tastes were strange to her, so strange as to be beyond her comprehension altogether. She found herself unable to argue with him because their minds were set on different planes, and her representations did not seem to touch him in the very least. And yet, after all, he was a very good boy, full of pure thoughts and kindly impulses and spiritual intuitions and intellectual proclivities which certainly no moralist would condemn. If only he were more practical, even more commonplace, and wouldn't talk such nonsense! Then there would not be such a gulf between them as there was at present; then she might have some influence over him for good, at any rate. Her thoughts recurred, uneasily, to the strange experiences of that morning. The mystery of the raps distracted her, puzzled her, frightened her; whereas Austin was not frightened at all—on the contrary, he accepted the whole thing with the serenest cheerfulness and *sang-froid*, finding it apparently quite natural that these unseen agencies, coming from nobody knew where, should take him under their protection and make friends with him. What could it all portend?

Of course it was very foolish of the good lady to fret like this because Austin was so different from what she thought he should be. She did not see that his nature was infinitely finer and subtler than her own, and that it was no use in the world attempting to stifle his intellectual growth and drag him down to her own level. A burly, muscular boy, who played football and read 'Tom Brown,' would have been far more to her taste, for such a one she would at least have understood. But Austin, with his queer notions and audacious paradoxes, was utterly beyond her. Unluckily, too, she had no sense of humour, and instead of laughing at his occasionally preposterous sallies, she allowed them to irritate and worry her. A person with no sense of humour is handicapped from start to finish, and is as much to be pitied as one born blind or deaf.

But Austin had his limitations too, and among them was a most deplorable want of tact. Otherwise he would never have said, as he was going to bed that night:

"By the way, auntie, what day have you arranged for the vicar to come and cast all those devils out of me?"

He might as well have let sleeping dogs lie. Aunt Charlotte turned round upon him in almost a rage, and solemnly forbade him, in any circumstances and under whatsoever provocation, ever to mention the subject in her presence again.

Chapter the Seventh

But by one of those curious coincidences that occur every now and then, who should happen to drop in the very next afternoon but the vicar himself, just as Austin and his aunt were having tea upon the lawn. Now Aunt Charlotte and the vicar were great friends. They had many interests in common—the same theological opinions, for example; and then Aunt Charlotte was indefatigable in all sorts of parish work, such as district-visiting, and the organisation of school teas, village clubs, and those rather formidable entertainments known as "treats"; so that the two had always something to talk about, and were very fond of meeting. Besides all this, there was another bond of union between them which scarcely anybody would have guessed. Mr Sheepshanks, though as unworldly a man as any in the county, considered himself unusually shrewd in business matters; and Aunt Charlotte, like many middle-aged ladies in her position, found it a great comfort to have a gentleman at her beck and call with whom she could talk confidentially about her investments, and who could be relied upon to give her much disinterested advice that he often acted on himself. On this particular afternoon the vicar hinted that he had something of special importance to communicate, and Aunt Charlotte was unusually gracious. He was a short gentleman, with a sloping forehead, a prominent nose, a clean-shaven, High-Church face, narrow, dogmatic views, and small, twinkling eyes; not the sort of person whom one would naturally associate with financial acumen, but endowed with an air of self-confidence, and a pretension to private information, which would have done credit to any stockbroker on 'Change.

"I've been thinking over that little matter of yours that you mentioned to me the other day," he began, when he had finished his third cup, and Austin had strolled away. "You say your mortgage at Southport has just been paid off, and you want a new investment for your money. Well, I think I know the very thing to suit you."

"Do you really? How kind of you!" exclaimed Aunt Charlotte. "What is it—shares or bonds?"

"Shares," replied Mr Sheepshanks; "shares. Of course I know that very prudent people will tell you that bonds are safer. And no doubt, as a rule they are. If a concern fails, the bond-holder is a creditor, while the shareholder is a debtor—besides having lost his capital. But in this case there is no fear of failure."

"Dear me," said Aunt Charlotte, beginning to feel impressed. "Is it an industrial undertaking?"

"I suppose it might be so described," answered her adviser, cautiously. "But it is mainly scientific. It is the outcome of a great chemical analysis."

"Oh, pray tell me all about it; I am so interested!" urged Aunt Charlotte, eagerly. "You know what confidence I have in your judgment. Has it anything to do with raw material? It isn't a plantation anywhere, is it?"

"It's gold!" said Mr Sheepshanks.

"Gold?" repeated Aunt Charlotte, rather taken aback. "A gold mine, I suppose you mean?"

"The hugest gold mine in the world," replied the vicar, enjoying her evident perplexity. "An inexhaustible gold mine. A gold mine without limits."

"But where—whereabouts is it?" cried Aunt Charlotte.

"All around you," said the vicar, waving his hands vaguely in the air. "Not in any country at all, but everywhere else. In the ocean."

"Gold in the ocean!" ejaculated the puzzled lady, dropping her knitting on her lap, and gazing helplessly at her financial mentor.

"Gold in the ocean—precisely," affirmed that gentleman in an impressive voice. "It has been discovered that seawater holds a large quantity of gold in solution, and that by some most interesting process of precipitation any amount of it can be procured ready for coining. I got a prospectus of the scheme this morning from Shark, Picaroon & Co., Fleece Court, London, and I've brought it for you to read. A most enterprising firm they seem to be. You'll see that it's full of very elaborate scientific details—the results of the analyses that have been made, the cost of production, estimates for machinery, and I don't know what all. I can't say I follow it very clearly myself, for the clerical mind, as everybody knows, is not very well adapted to grasping scientific terminology, but I can understand the general tenor of it well enough. It seems to me that the enterprise is promising in a very high degree."

"How very remarkable!" observed Aunt Charlotte, as she gazed at the tabulated figures and enumeration of chemical properties in bewildered awe. "And you think it a safe investment?"

"*I* do," replied Mr Sheepshanks, "but don't act on my opinion—judge for yourself. What's the amount you have to invest—two thousand pounds, isn't it? Well, I believe that you'd stand to get an income to that very amount by investing just that sum in the undertaking. Look what they say overleaf about the cost of working and the estimated returns. It all sounds fabulous, I admit, but there are the figures, my dear lady, in black and white, and figures cannot lie."

"I'll write to my bankers about it this very night," said Aunt Charlotte, folding up the prospectus and putting it carefully into her pocket. "It's evidently not a chance to be missed, and I'm most grateful to you, dear Mr Sheepshanks, for putting it in my way."

"Always delighted to be of service to you—as far as my poor judgment can avail," the vicar assured her with becoming modesty. "Ah, it's wonderful when one thinks of the teeming riches that lie around us, only waiting to be utilised. There *was* another scheme I thought of for you—a scheme for raising the sunken galleons in the Spanish main, and recovering the immense treasures that are now lying, safe and sound, at the bottom of the sea. Curious that both enterprises should be connected with salt water, eh? And the prospectus was headed with a most appropriate text—'The Sea shall give up her Dead.' That rather appealed to me, do you know. It cast an air of solemnity over the undertaking, and seemed to sanctify it somehow. However, I think the other will be the best. Well, Austin, and what are you reading now?"

"Aunt Charlotte's face," laughed Austin, sauntering up. "She looks as though you had been giving her absolution, Mr Sheepshanks—so beaming and refreshed. Why, what's it all about?"

"I expect you want more absolution than your aunt," said the vicar, humorously. "A sad useless fellow you are, I'm afraid. You and I must have a little serious talk together some day, Austin. I really want you to do something—for your own sake, you know. Now, how would you like to take a class in the Sunday-school, for instance? I shall have a vacancy in a week or two."

"Austin teach in the Sunday-school! He'd be more in his place if he went there as a scholar than as a teacher," said Aunt Charlotte, derisively.

"I don't know why you should say that," remarked Austin, with perfect gravity. "I think it would be delightful. I should make a beautiful Sunday-school teacher, I'm convinced."

"There, now!" exclaimed the vicar, approvingly.

Austin was standing under an apple tree, and over him stretched a horizontal branch laden with ripening fruit. He raised his hands on either side of his head and clasped it, and then began swinging his wooden leg round and round in a way that bade fair to get on Aunt Charlotte's nerves. He was so proud of that leg of his, while his aunt abhorred the very sight of it.

"No doubt they're all very charming boys, and I should love to tell them things," he went on. "I think I'd begin with 'The Gods of Greece'—Louis Dyer, you know—and then I'd read them a few carefully selected passages from the 'Phædrus.' Then, by way of something lighter, and more appropriate to their circumstances, I'd give them a course of Virgil—the 'Georgics', because, I suppose, most of them are connected with farming, and the 'Eclogues,' to initiate them into the poetical side of country life. When once I'd brought out all their latent sense of the Beautiful—for I'm afraid it *is* latent——"

"But it's a *Sunday*-school!" interrupted the vicar, horrified. "Virgil and the Phædrus indeed! My dear boy, have you taken leave of your senses? What in the world can you be thinking of?"

"Then what would you suggest?" enquired Austin, mildly.

"You'd have to teach them the Bible and the Catechism, of course," said Mr Sheepshanks, with an air of slight bewilderment.

"H'm—that seems to me rather a limited curriculum," replied Austin, dubiously. "I only remember one passage in the Catechism, beginning, 'My good child, know this.' I forget what it was he had to know, but it was something very dull. The Bible, of course, has more possibilities. There is some ravishing poetry in the Bible. Well, I can begin with the Bible, if you really prefer it, of course. The Song of Solomon, for instance. Oh, yes, that would be lovely! I'll divide it up into characters, and make each boy learn his part—the shepherd, the Shulamite, King Solomon, and all the rest of them. The Spring Song might even be set to music. And then all those lovely metaphors, about the two roes that were twins, and something else that was like a heap of wheat set about with lilies. Though, to be sure, I never could see any very striking resemblance between the objects typified and——"

"Hold your tongue, do, Austin!" cried Aunt Charlotte, scandalised. "And for mercy's sake, keep that leg of yours quiet, if you can. You are fidgeting me out of my wits."

Mr Sheepshanks, his mouth pursed up in a deprecating and uneasy smile, sat gazing vaguely in front of him. "I think it might be wise to defer the Song of Solomon," he suggested. "A few simple stories from the Book of Genesis, perhaps, would be better suited to the minds of your young pupils. And then the sublime opening chapters——"

"Oh, dear Mr Sheepshanks! Those stories in Genesis are some of them too *risqués* altogether," protested Austin. "One must draw the line somewhere, you see. We should be sure to come upon something improper, and just think how I should blush. Really, you can't expect me to read such things to boys actually younger than myself, and probably be asked to explain them into the bargain. There's the Creation part, it's true, but surely when one considers how occult all that is one wants to be familiar with the Kabbala and all sorts of mystical works to discover the hidden meaning. Now I should propose 'The Art of Creation'—do you know it? It shows that the only possible creator is Thought, and explains how everything exists in idea before it takes tangible shape. This applies to the universe at large, as well as to everything we make ourselves. I'd tell the boys that whenever they *think*, they are really *creating*, so that——"

"I should vastly like to know where you pick up all these extraordinary notions!" interrupted the vicar, who could not for the life of him make out whether Austin was in jest or earnest. "They're most dangerous notions, let me tell you, and entirely opposed to sound orthodox Church teaching. It's clear to me that your reading wants to be supervised, Austin, by some judicious friend. There's an excellent little work I got a few days ago that I think you would like to see. It's called 'The Mission-field in Africa.' There you'll find a most remarkable account of all those heathen superstitions——"

"Where is Africa?" asked Austin, munching a leaf.

"There!" exclaimed Aunt Charlotte. "That's Austin all over. He'll talk by the hour together about a lot of outlandish nonsense that no sensible person ever heard of, and all the time he doesn't even know where Africa is upon the map. What is to be done with such a boy?"

"Well, I think we'll postpone the question of his teaching in the Sunday-school, at all events," remarked the vicar, who began to feel rather sorry that he had ever suggested it. "It's more than probable that his ideas would be over the children's heads, and come into collision with what they heard in church. Well, now I must be going. You'll think over that little matter we were speaking of?" he said, as he took a neighbourly leave of his parishioner and ally.

"Indeed I will, and I'll write to my bankers tonight," replied that lady cordially.

Then the vicar ambled across the lawn, and Austin accompanied him, as in duty bound, to the garden gate. Meanwhile, Aunt Charlotte leant comfortably back in her wicker chair, absorbed in pleasant meditation. The repairs to the roof would, no doubt, run into a little money, but the vicar's tip about this wonderful company for extracting gold from seawater made up for any anxiety she might otherwise have experienced upon that score. What a kind, good man he was—and *so* clever in business matters, which, of course, were out of her range altogether. She took the prospectus out of her pocket, and ran her eyes over it again. Capital, £500,000, in shares of £100 each. Solicitors, Messrs Somebody Something & Co., Fetter Lane, E.C. Bankers, The Shoreditch & Houndsditch Amalgamated Banking Corporation, St Mary Axe. Acquisition of machinery, so much. Cost of working, so much. Estimated returns—something perfectly enormous. It all looked wonderful, quite wonderful. She again determined to write to her bankers that very evening before dinner.

"You're going to the theatre tonight, aren't you, Austin?" she said, as he returned from seeing Mr Sheepshanks courteously off the premises. "I want you to post a letter for me on your way. Post it at the Central Office, so as to be sure it catches the night mail. It's a business letter of importance."

"All right, auntie," he replied, arranging his trouser so that it should fall gracefully over his wooden leg.

"And I do wish, Austin, that you'd behave rather more like other people when Mr Sheepshanks comes to see us. There really is no necessity for talking to him in the way you do. Of course it was a great compliment, his asking you to take a class in the Sunday-school, though I could have told him that he couldn't possibly have made an absurder choice, and you might very well have contented yourself with regretting your utter unfitness for such a post without exposing your ignorance in the way you did. The idea of telling a clergyman, too, that the Book of Genesis was too improper for boys to read, when he had just been recommending it! I thought you'd have had more respect for his position, whatever silly notions you may have yourself."

"I do respect the vicar; he's quite a nice little thing," replied Austin, in a conciliatory tone. "And of course he thinks just what a vicar ought to think, and I suppose what all vicars do think. But as I'm not a vicar myself I don't see that I am bound to think as they do."

"You a vicar, indeed!" sniffed Aunt Charlotte. "A remarkable sort of vicar you'd make, and pretty sermons you'd preach if you had the chance. What time does this performance of yours begin tonight?"

"At eight, I believe."

"Well, then, I'll just go in and tell cook to let us have dinner a quarter of an hour earlier than usual," said Aunt Charlotte, as she folded up her work. "The omnibus from the 'Peacock' will get you into town in plenty of time, and the walk back afterwards will do you good."

*   *   *

The town in question was about a couple of miles from the village where Austin lived—a clean, cheerful, prosperous little borough, with plenty of good shops, a commodious theatre, several churches and chapels, and a fine market. Dinner was soon disposed of, and as the omnibus which plied between the two places clattered and rattled along at a good speed—having to meet the seven-fifty down-train at the railway station—he was able to post his aunt's precious letter and slip into his stall in the dress-circle before the curtain rose. The orchestra was rioting through a composition called 'The Clang o' the Wooden Shoon,' as an appropriate introduction to a tragedy the scene of which was laid in Nineveh; the house seemed fairly full, and the air was heavy with that peculiar smell, a sort of doubtfully aromatic stuffiness, which is so grateful to the nostrils of playgoers. Austin gazed around him with keen interest. He had not been inside a theatre for years, and the vivid description that Mr Buskin had given him of the show he was about to witness filled him with pleasurable anticipation. To all intents and purposes, the experience that awaited him was something entirely new; how, he wondered, would it fit into his scheme of life? What room would there be, in his idealistic philosophy, for the stage?

Then the music came to an end in a series of defiant bangs, the curtain rolled itself out of sight, and a brilliant spectacle appeared. The only occupant of the scene at first was a gentleman in a thick black beard and fantastic garb who seemed to have acquired the habit of talking very loudly to himself. In this way the audience discovered that the gentleman, who was no less a personage than the Queen's brother, was seriously dissatisfied with his royal brother-in-law, whose habits were of a nature which did not make for the harmony of his domestic circle. Then soft music was heard, and in lounged Sardanapalus himself—a glittering figure in flowing robes of silver and pale blue, garlanded with flowers, and surrounded by a crowd of slaves and women all very elegantly dressed; and it really was quite wonderful to notice how his Majesty lolled and languished about the stage, how beautifully affected all his gestures were, and with what a highbred supercilious drawl he rolled out his behests that a supper should be served at midnight in the pavilion that commanded a view of the Euphrates. And this magnificent, absurd creature—this mouthing, grimacing, attitudinising popinjay, thought Austin, was no other than Mr Bucephalus Buskin, with whom he had chatted on easy terms in a common field only a few days previously! The memory of the umbrella, the tight frock-coat, the bald head, the fat, reddish face, and the rather rusty "chimney-pot" here recurred to him, and he nearly giggled out loud in thinking how irresistibly funny Mr Buskin would look if he were now going through all these fanciful gesticulations in his walking dress. The fact was that the man himself was perfectly unrecognisable, and Austin was mightily impressed by what was really a signal triumph in the art of making up.

The play went on, and Sardanapalus showed no signs of moral improvement. In fact, it soon became evident that his code of ethics was deplorable, and Austin could only console himself with the thought that the real Mr Buskin was, no doubt, a most virtuous and respectable person who never gave Mrs Buskin—if there was one—any grounds for jealousy. Then the first act came to an end, the lights went up, and a subdued buzz of conversation broke out all over the theatre. The second act was even more exciting, as Sardanapalus, having previously confessed himself unable to go on multiplying empires, was forced to interfere in a scuffle between his brother-in-law and Arbaces—who was by way of being a traitor; but the most sensational scene of all was the banquet in act the third, of which so glowing an account had been given to Austin by the great tragedian himself. That, indeed, was something to remember.

"Guests, to my pledge!
Down on your knees, and drink a measure to
The safety of the King—the monarch, say I?
The god Sardanapalus! mightier than
His father Baal, the god Sardanapalus!"
[Thunder. Confusion.]

Ah, that was thrilling, if you like, in spite of the halting rhythm. And yet, even at that supreme moment, the vision of the umbrella and the rather shabby hat would crop up again, and Austin didn't quite know whether to let himself be thrilled or to lean back and roar. The conspiracy burst out a few minutes afterwards, and then there ensued a most terrifying and portentous battle, rioters and loyalists furiously attempting to kill each other by the singular expedient of clattering their swords together so as to make as much noise as possible, and then passing them under their antagonists' armpits, till the stage was heaped with corpses; and all this bloody work entirely irrespective of the valuable glass and china on the supper-table, and the costly hearthrugs strewn about the floor. Even Sardanapalus, having first looked in the glass to make sure that his helmet was straight, performed prodigies of valour, and the curtain descended to his insatiable shouting for fresh weapons and a torrent of tumultuous applause from the gallery.

"Now for it!" said Austin to himself, when another act had been got through, in the course of which Sardanapalus had suffered from a distressing nightmare. He took Mr Buskin's card out of his pocket, and, hurrying out as fast as he could manage, stumped his way round to the stage door. Cerberus would fain have stopped him, but Austin flourished his card in passing, and enquired of the first civil-looking man he met where the manager was to be found. He was piloted through devious ways and under strange scaffoldings, to the foot of a steep and very dirty flight of steps—luckily there were only seven—at the top of which was dimly visible a door; and at this, having screwed his courage to the sticking-place, he knocked.

"Come in!" cried a voice inside.

He found himself on the threshold of a room such as he had never seen before. There was no carpet, and the little furniture it contained was heaped with masses of heterogeneous clothes. Two looking-glasses were fixed against the walls, and in front of one of them was a sort of shelf, or dresser, covered with small pots of some ungodly looking materials of a pasty appearance—rouge, grease-paint, cocoa-butter, and heaven knows what beside—with black stuff, white stuff, yellow stuff, paintbrushes, gum-pots, powderpuffs, and discoloured rags spread about in not very picturesque confusion. In a corner of this engaging boudoir, sitting in an armchair with a glass of liquor beside him and smoking a strong cigar, was the most extraordinary and repulsive object he had ever clapped his eyes on. The face, daubed and glistening with an unsightly coating of red, white, and yellow-ochre paint, and adorned with protuberant bristles by way of eyebrows, appeared twice its natural dimensions. The throat was bare to the collarbones. A huge wig covered the head, falling over the shoulders; while the whole was encircled by a great wreath of pink calico roses, the back of which, just under the nape of the neck, was fastened by a glittering pinchbeck tassel. The arms were nude, their natural growth of dark hair being plastered over with white chalk, which had a singularly ghastly effect; a short-skirted, low-necked gold frock, cut like a little girl's, partly covered the body, and over this were draped coarse folds of scarlet, purple, and white, with tinsel stars along the seams, and so disposed as to display to fullest advantage the brawny calves of the tragedian.

"Great Scott, if it isn't young Dot-and-carry-One!" exclaimed Mr Sardanapalus Buskin, as the slim figure of Austin, in his simple evening-dress, appeared at the entrance. "Come in, young gentleman, come in. So you've come to beard the lion in his den, have you? Well, it's kind of you not to have forgotten. You're welcome, very welcome. That was a very pleasant little meeting we had the other day, over there in the fields. And what do you think of the performance? Been in front?"

"Oh, yes—thank you so very much," said Austin, hesitatingly. "It is awfully kind of you to let me come and see you like this. I've never seen anything of the sort in all my life."

"Ah, I daresay it's a sort of revelation to you," said Sardanapalus, with good-humoured condescension. "Have a drop of whiskey-and-water? Well, well, I won't press you. And so you've enjoyed the play?"

"The whole thing has interested me enormously," replied Austin. "It has given me any amount to think of."

"Ah, that's good; that's very good, indeed," said the actor, nodding sagely. "Do you remember what I was saying to you the other day about the educative power of the stage? That's what it is, you see; the greatest educative power in the land. How did that last scene go? Made the people in the stalls sit up a bit, I reckon. Ah, it's a great life, this. Talk of art! I tell you, young gentleman, acting's the only art worthy of the name. The actor's all the artists in creation rolled into one. Every art that exists conspires to produce him and to perfect him. Painting, for instance; did you ever see anything to compare with that Banqueting Scene in the Palace? Why, it's a triumph of pictorial art, and, by Jove, of architecture too. And the actor doesn't only paint scenes—or get them painted for him, it comes to the same thing—he paints himself. Look at me, for instance. Why, I could paint you, young gentleman, so that your own mother wouldn't know you. With a few strokes of the brush I could transform you into a beautiful young girl, or a wrinkled old Jew, or an Artful Dodger, or anything else you had a fancy for. Music, again—think of the effect of that slow music in the first act. There was pathos for you, if you like. Oratory—talk of Demosthenes or Cicero, Mr Gladstone or John Bright! Why, they're nowhere, my dear young friend, literally nowhere. Didn't my description of the dream just *fetch* you? Be honest now; by George, Sir, it thrilled the house. Look here, young man"—and Sardanapalus began to speak very slowly, with tremendous emphasis and solemnity—"and remember what I'm going to say until your dying day. If I were to drink too much of this, I should be intoxicated; but what is the intoxication produced by whiskey compared with the intoxication of applause? Just think of it, as soberly and calmly as you can—hundreds of people, all in their right minds, stamping and shouting and yelling for you to come and show yourself before the curtain; the entire house at your feet. Why, it's worship, Sir, sheer worship; and worship is a very sacred thing. Show me the man who's superior to *that*, and I'll show you a man who's either above or below the level of human nature. Whatever he may be, I don't envy him. To-morrow morning I shall be an ordinary citizen in a frock-coat and a tall hat. To-night I'm a king, a god. What other artist can say as much?"

So saying, Sardanapalus puffed up his cigar and swallowed another half glass of liquor. The pungent smoke made Austin cough and blink. "It must indeed be an exciting life," he ventured; "quite delirious, to judge from what you say."

"It requires a cool head," replied Sardanapalus, with a stoical shrug. "Ah! there's the bell," he added, as a loud ting was heard outside. "The curtain's going up. Now hurry away to the front, and see the last act. The scene where I'm burnt on the top of all my treasures isn't to be missed. It's the grandest and most moving scene in any play upon the stage. And watch the expression of my face," said Mr Buskin, as he applied the powderpuff to his cheeks and nose. "Gestures are all very well—any fool can be taught to act with his arms and legs. But expression! That's where the heaven-born genius comes in. However, I must be off. Good-night, young gentleman, good-night."

He shook Austin warmly by the hand, and precipitated himself down the wooden steps. Austin followed, regained the stage door, and was soon back in the dress-circle. But he felt that really he had seen almost enough. The last act seemed to drag, and it was only for the sake of witnessing the holocaust at the end that he sat it out. Even the varying "expressions" assumed by Sardanapalus failed to arouse his enthusiasm. He reproached himself for this, for poor Buskin rolled his eyes and twisted his mouth and pulled such lugubrious faces that Austin felt how pathetic it all was, and how hard the man was trying to work upon the feelings of the audience. But the flare-up at the end was really very creditable. Blue fire, red fire, and clouds of smoke filled the entire stage, and when Myrrha clambered up the burning pile to share the fate of her paramour the enthusiasm of the spectators knew no bounds. Calls for Sardanapalus and all his company resounded from every part of the house, and it was a tremendous moment when the curtain was drawn aside, and the great actor, apparently not a penny the worse for having just been burnt alive, advanced majestically to the footlights. Then all the other performers were generously permitted to approach and share in the ovation, bowing again and again in acknowledgment of the approbation of their patrons, and looking, thought Austin rather cruelly, exactly like a row of lacqueys in masquerade. This marked the close of the proceedings, and Austin, with a sigh of relief, soon found himself once more in the cool streets, walking briskly in the direction of the country.

Well, he had had his experience, and now his curiosity was satisfied. What was the net result? He began sifting his sensations, and trying to discover what effect the things he had seen and heard had really had upon him. It was all very brilliant, very interesting; in a certain way, very exciting. He began to understand what it was that made so many people fond of theatregoing. But he felt at the same time that he himself was not one of them. For some reason or other he had escaped the spell. He was more inclined to criticise than to enjoy. There was something wanting in it all. What could that something be?

The sound of footsteps behind him, echoing in the quiet street, just then reached his ears. The steps came nearer, and the next moment a well-known voice exclaimed:

"Well, Austin! I hoped I should catch you up!"

"Oh, Mr St Aubyn, is that you? How glad I am to see you!" cried the boy, grasping the other's hand. "This is a delightful surprise. Have you been to the theatre, too?"

"I have," replied St Aubyn. "You didn't notice me, I daresay, but I was watching you most of the time. It amused me to speculate what impression the thing was making on you. Were you very much carried away?"

"I certainly was not," said Austin, "though I was immensely interested. It gave me a lot to think about, as I told Mr Buskin himself when I went to see him for a few minutes behind the scenes. You know I happened to meet him a few days ago, and he asked me to—it really was most kind of him. By the way, he was just on his way to call upon you at the Court."

"Well—and now tell me what you thought of it all. What impressed you most about the whole affair?"

"I think," said Austin, speaking very slowly, as though weighing every word, "that the general impression made upon me was that of utter unreality. I cannot conceive of anything more essentially artificial. The music was pretty, the scenery was very fine, and the costumes were dazzling enough—from a distance; but when you've said that you've said everything. The situations were impossible and absurd. The speeches were bombast. The sentiment was silly and untrue. And Sardanapalus himself was none so distraught by his unpleasant dream and all his other troubles but that he was looking forward to his glass of whiskey-and-water between the acts. No, he didn't impose on me one bit. I didn't believe in Sardanapalus for a moment, even before I had the privilege of seeing and hearing him as Mr Buskin in his dressing-room. The entire business was a sham."

"But surely it doesn't pretend to be anything else?" suggested St Aubyn, surprised.

"Be it so. I don't like shams, I suppose," returned the boy.

"Still, you shouldn't generalise too widely," urged the other. "There are plays where one's sensibilities are really touched, where the situations are not forced, where the performers move and speak like living, ordinary human beings, and, in the case of great actors, work upon the feelings of the audience to such an extent——"

"And there the artificiality is all the greater!" chipped in Austin, tersely. "The more perfect the illusion, the hollower the artificiality. Of course, no one could take Sardanapalus seriously, any more than if he were a marionette pulled by strings instead of the sort of live marionette he really is. But where the acting and the situations are so perfect, as you say, as to cause real emotion, the unreality of the whole business is more flagrantly conspicuous than ever. The emotions pourtrayed are not real, and nobody pretends they are. The art, therefore, of making them appear real, and even communicating them to the audience, must of necessity involve greater artificiality than where the acting is bad and the situations ridiculous. There's a person I know, near where I live—you never heard of him, of course, but he's called Jock MacTavish—and he told me he once went to see a really very great actress do some part or other in which she had to die a most pathetic death. It was said to be simply heartrending, and everybody used to cry. Well, the night Jock MacTavish was there something went wrong—a sofa was out of its place, or a bolster had been forgotten, or a rope wouldn't work, I don't know what it was—and the language that woman indulged in while she was in the act of dying would have disgraced a bargee. Jock was in a stage-box and heard every filthy word of it. Of course *he* told me the story as a joke, and I was rather disgusted, but I'm glad he did so now. That was an extreme case, I know—such things don't occur one time in ten thousand, no doubt—but it's an illustration of what I mean when I say that the finer the illusion produced the hollower the sham that produces it."

"You're a mighty subtle-minded young person for your age," exclaimed St Aubyn, with a good-humoured laugh. "I confess that your theory is new to me; it had never occurred to me before. For one who has only been inside a theatre two or three times in his life you seem to have elaborated your conclusions pretty quickly. I may infer, then, that you're not exactly hankering to go on the stage yourself?"

"*I?*" said Austin, drawing himself up. "I, disguise myself in paint and feathers to be a public gazing-stock? Of course you mean it as a joke."

"And yet there *are* gentlemen upon the stage," observed St Aubyn, in order to draw him on.

"So much the better for the stage, perhaps; so much the worse for the gentlemen," replied Austin haughtily.

A pause. They were now well out in the open country, with the moonlit road stretching far in front of them. Then St Aubyn said, in a different tone altogether:

"You surprise me beyond measure by what you say. I should have thought that a boy of your poetical and artistic temperament would have had his imagination somewhat fired, even by the efforts of the poor showman whom we've seen tonight. Now I will make you a confession. At the bottom of my heart I agree with every word you've said. I may be one-sided, prejudiced, what you will, but I cannot help looking upon a public performer as I look upon no other human being. And I pity the performer, too; he takes himself so seriously, he fails so completely to realise what he really is. And the danger of going on the stage is that, once an actor, always an actor. Let a man once get bitten by the craze, and there's no hope for him. Only the very finest natures can escape. The fascination is too strong. He's ruined for any other career, however honourable and brilliant."

"Is that so, really?" asked Austin. "I cannot see where all this wonderful fascination comes in. I should think it must be a dreadful trade myself."

"So it is. Because they don't know it. Because of the very fascination which exists, although you can't understand it. Let me tell you a story. I knew a man once upon a time—he was a great friend of mine—in the navy. Although he was quite young, not more than twenty-six, he was already a distinguished officer; he had seen active service, been mentioned in despatches, and all the rest of it. He was also, curiously enough, a most accomplished botanist, and had written papers on the flora of Cambodia and Yucatan that had been accepted with marked appreciation by the Linnæan Society. Well—that man, who had a brilliant career before him, and would probably have been an admiral and a K.C.B. if he had stuck to it, got attacked by the theatrical microbe. He chucked everything, and devoted his whole life to acting. He is acting still. He cares for nothing else. It is the one and only thing in the universe he lives for. The service of his country, the pure fame of scientific research and authorship, are as nothing to him, the merest dust in the balance, as compared with the cheap notoriety of the footlights."

"He must be mad. And is he a success?" asked Austin.

"Judge for yourself—you've just been seeing him," replied St Aubyn. "Though, of course, his name is no more Buskin than yours or mine."

"Good Heavens!" cried the boy. "And Mr Buskin was—all that?"

"He was all that," responded the other. "It was rather painful for me to see him this evening in his present state, as you may imagine. As to his being successful in a monetary sense, I really cannot tell you. But, to do him justice, I don't think he cares for money in the very least. So long as he makes two ends meet he's quite satisfied. All he cares about is painting his face, and dressing himself up, and ranting, and getting rounds of applause. And, so far, he certainly has his reward. His highest ambition, it is true, he has not yet attained. If he could only get his portrait published in a halfpenny paper wearing some new-shaped stock or collar that the hosiers were anxious to bring into fashion, he would feel that there was little left to live for. But that is a distinction reserved for actors who stand at the tip-top of their profession, and I'm afraid that poor Buskin has but little chance of ever realising his aspiration."

"Are you serious?" said Austin, open-eyed.

"Absolutely," replied St Aubyn. "I know it for a fact."

"Well," exclaimed Austin, fetching a deep breath, "of course if a man has to do this sort of thing for a living—if it's his only way of making money—I don't think I despise him so much. But if he does it because he loves it, loves it better than any other earthly thing, then I despise him with all my heart and soul. I cannot conceive a more utterly unworthy existence."

"And to such an existence our friend Buskin has sacrificed his whole career," replied St Aubyn, gravely.

"What a tragedy," observed the boy.

"Yes; a tragedy," agreed the other. "A truer tragedy than the imitation one that he's been acting in, if he could only see it. Well, here is my turning. Good-night! I'm very glad we met. Come and see me soon. I'm not going away again."

Then Austin, left alone, stumped thoughtfully along the country road. The sweet smell of the flowery hedges pervaded the night air, and from the fields on either side was heard ever and anon the bleating of some wakeful sheep. How peaceful, how reposeful, everything was! How strong and solemn the great trees looked, standing here and there in the wide meadows under the moonlight and the stars! And what a contrast—oh, *what* a contrast—was the beauty of these calm pastoral scenes to the tawdry gorgeousness of those other "scenes" he had been witnessing, with their false effects, and coloured fires, and painted, spouting occupants! There was no need for him to argue the question any more, even with himself. It was as clear as the moon in the steel-blue sky above him that the associations of the theatre were totally, hopelessly, and radically incompatible with the ideals of the Daphnis life.

Chapter the Eighth

It is scarcely necessary to say that Austin knew nothing whatever about his aunt's preoccupation, and that even if she had taken him into her confidence, he would have paid little or no attention to the matter. I am afraid that his ideas about finance were crude in the extreme, being limited to a sort of vague impression that capital was what you put into a bank, and interest was what you took out; while the difference between the par value of a security and the price you could get for it on the market, would have been to him a hopelessly unfathomable mystery. Aunt Charlotte, therefore, was very wise in abstaining from any reference, in conversation, to the great enterprise for extracting gold from seawater, in which she hoped to purchase shares; for one could never have told what foolish remark he might have made, though it was quite certain that he would have said something foolish, and probably very exasperating. So she kept her secret locked up in her own breast, and silently counted the hours till she could get a reply from her bankers.

Of course Austin had to give his aunt an account, at breakfast-time next morning, of the pageant of the previous night; and as he confined himself to saying that the scenery and dresses were very fine, and that Mr Buskin was quite unrecognisable, and that all the performers knew their parts, and that he had walked part of the way home with Roger St Aubyn afterwards, the impression left on the good lady's mind was that he had enjoyed himself very much. This inevitable duty accomplished, Austin straightway banished the whole subject from his memory and gave himself up more unreservedly than ever to his garden and his thoughts. How fresh and sweet and welcoming the garden looked on that calm, lovely summer day! How brightly the morning dewdrops twinkled on the leaves, like a sprinkling of liquid diamonds! Every flower seemed to greet him with silent laughter: "Aha, you've been playing truant, have you? Straying into alien precincts, roving in search of something newer and gaudier than anything you have here? Sunlight palls on you; gas is so much more festive! The scents of the fields are vulgar; finer the hot smells of the playhouse, more meet for a cultured nostril!" Of course Austin made all this nonsense up himself, but he felt so happy that it amused him to attribute the words to the dear flower-friends who were all around him, and to whom he could never be really faithless. Faugh! that playhouse! He would never enter one again. Be an actor! Lubin was a cleaner gentleman than any painted Buskin on the stage. Here, in the clear, pure splendour of the sunlit air, the place where he had been last night loomed up in his consciousness as something meretricious and unwholesome. Yet he was glad he had been, for it made everything so much purer and sweeter by contrast. Never had the garden looked more meetly set, never had the sun shone more genially, and the air impelled the blood and sent it coursing more joyously through his veins, than on that morning of the rejuvenescence of all his high ideals.

Then he drew a small blue volume out of his pocket, and lay down on the grass with his back against the trunk of an apple tree. Austin's theory—or one of his theories, for he had hundreds—was that one's literature should always be in harmony with one's surroundings; and so, intending to pass his morning in the garden, he had chosen 'The Garden of Cyrus' as an appropriate study. He opened it reverently, for it was compact of jewelled thoughts that had been set to words by one of the princes of prose. He, the young garden-lover, sat at the feet of the great garden-mystic, and began to pore wonderingly over the inscrutable secrets of the quincunx. His fine ear was charmed by the rhythm of the sumptuous and stately sentences, and his pulses throbbed in response to every measured phrase in which the lore of garden symmetry and the principles of garden science were set forth. He read of the hanging gardens of Babylon, first made by Queen Semiramis, third or fourth from Nimrod, and magnificently renewed by Nabuchodonosor, according to Josephus: *"from whence, overlooking Babylon, and all the region about it, he found no circumscription to the eye of his ambition; till, over-delighted with the bravery of this Paradise, in his melancholy metamorphosis he found the folly of that delight, and a proper punishment in the contrary habitation—in wild plantations and wanderings of the fields."* Austin shook his head over this; he did not think it possible to love a garden too much, and demurred to the idea that such a love deserved any punishment at all. But that was theology, and he had no taste for theological dissertations. So he dipped into the pages where the quincunx is "naturally" considered, and here he admired the encyclopædic learning of the author, which appeared to have been as wide as that attributed to Solomon; then glanced at the "mystic" part, which he reserved for later study. But one paragraph riveted his attention, as he turned over the leaves. Here was a mine of gold, a treasure-house of suggestiveness and wisdom.

*"Light, that makes things seen, makes some things invisible;
were it not for darkness and the shadow of the earth, the noblest
part of the creation had remained unseen, and the stars in heaven
as invisible as on the fourth day, when they were created above the
horizon with the sun, or there was not an eye to behold them. The
greatest mystery of religion is expressed by adumbration, and in
the noblest part of Jewish types, we find the cherubim shadowing
the mercy-seat. Life itself is but the shadow of death, and souls
departed but the shadows of the living. All things fall under this
name. The sun itself is but the dark simulacrum, and light but the
shadow of God."*

Austin delighted in symbolism, and these apparent paradoxes fascinated him. But was it all true? He loved to think that
life was the shadow, and death—what we call death—the substance; he had always felt that the reality of everything was to be
sought for on the other side. But he could not see why departed
souls should be regarded as the shadows of living men. Rather it
was we who lived in a vain show, and would continue to do so until
the spirit, the true substance of us, should be set free. Well, whatever the truth of it might be, it was all a charming puzzle, and we
should learn all about it some day, and meantime he had been fur-
nished with an entirely new idea—the revealing power of darkness. He loved the light because it was beautiful, and now he
loved the darkness because it was mysterious, and held such won-
drous secrets in its folds. He had never been afraid of the dark
even when a child. It had always been associated in his mind with
sleep and dreams, and he was very fond of both.

Of course it would have been no use attempting to instruct
Lubin in the cryptic properties of the quincunx, or any other theories of garden arrangement propounded by Sir Thomas Browne.
And Aunt Charlotte would have proved a still more hopeless subject. She had no head for mysticism, poor dear, and Austin often
told her she was one of the greatest sceptics he had ever known.
"You believe in nothing but your dinner, your bankbook, and your
Bible, auntie; I declare it's perfectly shocking," he said to her one
day. "And a very good creed too," she replied; "it wouldn't be a bad
thing for you either, if you had a little more sound religion and
practical common-sense." Just now it was the bankbook phase
that was uppermost, and when a letter was brought in to her at
breakfast-time next morning bearing the London postmark, she
clutched it eagerly and opened it with evident anticipation. But as
she read the contents her brow clouded and her face fell. Clearly

she was disappointed and surprised, but made no remark to Austin.

A couple of days passed without anything of importance happening, except that she wrote again to her bankers and looked out anxiously for their reply. But none came, and she grew irritable and disturbed. It really was most extraordinary; she had always thought that bankers were so shrewd, and prompt, and businesslike, and yet here they were, treating her as though she were of no account whatever, and actually leaving her second letter without an answer. The affair was pressing, too. There was certain to be a perfect rush for shares in so exceptional an undertaking, and when once they were all allotted, of course up they'd go to an enormous premium, and all her chances of investing would be lost. It was too exasperating for words. What were the men thinking of? Why were they so neglectful of her interests? She had always been an excellent customer, and had never overdrawn her account—never. And now they were leaving her in the lurch. However, she determined she would not submit. She fumed in silence for yet another day, and then, at dinner in the evening, came out with a most unexpected declaration.

"Austin," she said suddenly, after a long pause, "I'm going to town tomorrow by the 10:27 train."

Austin was peeling an apple, intent on seeing how long a strip he could pare off without breaking it. "Won't it be very hot?" he asked absently.

"Hot? Well, perhaps it will," said Aunt Charlotte, rather nettled at his indifference. "But I can't help that. The fact is that my bankers are giving me a great deal of annoyance just now, and I'm going up to London to have it out with them."

"Really?" replied Austin, politely interested. "I hope they haven't been embezzling your money?"

"Do, for goodness sake, pull yourself together and try not to talk nonsense for once in your life," retorted Aunt Charlotte, tartly. "Embezzling my money, indeed!—I should just like to catch them at it. Of course it's nothing of the kind. But I've lately given them certain instructions which they virtually refuse to carry out, and in a case of that sort it's always better to discuss the affair in person."

"I see," said Austin, beginning to munch his apple. "I wonder why they won't do what you want them to. Isn't it very rude of them?"

"Rude? Well—I can't say they've been exactly rude," acknowledged Aunt Charlotte. "But they're making all sorts of difficulties, and hint that they know better than I do——"

"Which is absurd, of course," put in Austin, with his very simplest air.

Aunt Charlotte glanced sharply at him, but there was not the faintest trace of irony in his expression. "I fancy they don't quite understand the question," she said, "so I intend to run up and explain it to them. One can do these things so much better in conversation than by writing. I shall get lunch in town, and then there'll be time for me to do a little shopping, perhaps, before catching the 4:40 back. That will get me here in ample time for dinner at half past seven."

"And what train do you go by in the morning?" enquired Austin.

"The 10:27," replied his aunt. "I shall take the omnibus from the Peacock that starts at a quarter to ten."

It cannot be said that Aunt Charlotte's projected trip to town interested Austin much. Business of any sort was a profound mystery to him, and with regard to speculations, investments, and such-like matters his mind was a perfect blank. He had a vague notion that perhaps Aunt Charlotte wanted some money, and that the bankers had refused to give her any; though whether she had a right to demand it, or they a right to withhold it, he had no more idea than the man in the moon. So he dismissed the whole affair from his mind as something with which he had nothing whatever to do, and spent the evening in the company of Sir Thomas Browne. At ten o'clock he went forth into the garden, and became absorbed in an attempt to identify the different colours of the flowers in the moonlight. It proved a fascinating occupation, for the pale, cold brightness imparted hues to the flowers that were strange and weird, so that it was a matter of real difficulty to say what the colours actually were. Then he wondered how it was he had never before discovered what an inspiring thing it was to wander all alone at night about a garden illuminated by a brilliant moon. The shadows were so black and secret, the radiance so spiritual, the shapes so startlingly fantastic, it was like being in another world. And then the silence. That was the most compelling charm of all. It helped him to feel. And he felt that he was not alone, though he heard nothing and saw nobody. The garden was full of flower-fairies, invisible elves and sprites whose mission it was to guard the flowers, and who loved the moonlight more than they loved the day; dainty, diaphanous creatures who were wafted across the smooth lawns on summer breezes, and washed the thirsty petals and drooping leaves in the dew which the clear blue air of night diffuses so abundantly. He had a sense—almost a knowledge—that the garden he was in was a dream-garden, a sort of panoramic phantasm, and that the real garden lay *behind* it somehow, hidden from material eyesight, eluding material touch, but there all the same, unearthly and elysian, more beautiful a great deal than the one in which he was standing, and teeming with gracious presences. It seemed a revelation to him, this sudden perception of a real world underlying the apparent one; and for nearly half-an-hour he sauntered to and fro in a reverie, leaning sometimes against the old stone fountain, and sometimes watching the pale clouds as they began flitting together as though to keep a rendezvous in space, until they concealed the face of the moon entirely from view and left the garden dark.

*　　　*　　　*

Whether Austin had strange dreams that night or no, certain it is that when he came down to breakfast in the morning his face was set and there was a look of unusual preoccupation in his eyes. Aunt Charlotte, being considerably preoccupied with her own affairs, noticed nothing, and busied herself with the teapot as was her wont. Austin chipped his egg in silence, while his auntie, helping herself generously to fried bacon, made some remark about the desirability of laying a good foundation in view of her journey up to town. Thereupon Austin said:

"Is it absolutely necessary for you to go to town this morning, auntie?"

"Of course it is," replied Aunt Charlotte, munching heartily. "I told you so last night."

"Why can't you go tomorrow instead?" asked Austin, tentatively. "Would it be too late?"

"I've arranged to go *today*," said Aunt Charlotte, with decision. "The sooner this business is settled the better. What should I gain by waiting?"

"I don't see any particular hurry," said Austin. "It's only giving yourself trouble for nothing. If I were you I'd write what you want to say, and then go up to see these people if their answer was still unsatisfactory."

"But you see you don't know anything about the matter," retorted Aunt Charlotte, beginning to wonder at the boy's persistency. "What in the world makes you want me not to go?"

"Oh—I only thought it might prove unnecessary," replied he, rather lamely. "It's going to be very hot, and after all——"

"It'll be quite as hot tomorrow," said Aunt Charlotte, as she stirred her tea.

"Well, why not go by a later train, then?" suggested Austin. "Look here; go by the 4:20 this afternoon, and take me with you. We'll go to a nice quiet hotel, and have a beautiful dinner, and see some of the sights, and then you'd have all tomorrow morning to do your business with these horrid old gentlemen at the bank. Now don't you think that's rather a good idea?"

"I—dare—*say!*" cried Aunt Charlotte, in her highest key. "So that's what you're aiming at, is it? Oh, you're a cunning boy, my dear, if ever there was one. But your little project would cost at least four times as much as I propose to spend today, and for that reason alone it's not to be thought of for a moment. What in creation ever put such an idea into your head?"

"I don't want to come with you in the very least, really—especially as you don't want to have me," replied Austin. "But I do wish you'd give up your idea of going to London by the 10:27 this morning. If you'll only do that I don't care for anything else. Take the same train tomorrow, if you like, but not today. That's all I have to ask you."

"But why—why—why?" demanded Aunt Charlotte, in not unnatural amazement.

"I can't tell you why," said Austin. "It wouldn't be any use."

"You are the very absurdest child I ever came across!" exclaimed Aunt Charlotte. "I've often had to put up with your fancies, but never with any so outrageously unreasonable as this. Now not another word. I'm going to travel by the 10:27 this morning, and if you like to come and see me off, you're at perfect liberty to do so."

Austin made no reply, and breakfast proceeded in silence. Then he glanced at the clock, and saw that it was ten minutes to nine. As soon as the meal was finished, he rose from his chair and moved slowly towards the door.

"You still intend to go by the——"

"Hold your tongue!" snapped his aunt. Whereupon Austin left the room without another word. Then he stumped his way upstairs and was not seen again. Aunt Charlotte, meanwhile, began preparations for her journey. It was now close on nine o'clock, and she had to order the dinner, see that she had sufficient money for her expenses, choose a bonnet for travelling in, and look after half a dozen other important trifles before setting out to catch the railway omnibus at the Peacock. At last Austin, waiting behind a door, heard her enter her room to dress. Very gently he stole out with something in his pocket, and two minutes afterwards was standing on the lawn with his straw hat tilted over his eyes, chattering with Lubin about tubers, corms, and bulbs, potting and bedding-out, and other pleasant mysteries of garden-craft.

It was not very long, however, before a singular bustle was heard on the first floor. Maids ran scuttling up and down stairs, voices resounded through the open windows, and then came the sound of thumps, as of somebody vigorously battering at a door. Austin turned round, and began walking towards the house. He was met by old Martha, who seemed to be in a tremendous fluster about something.

"Master Austin! Master Austin! Oh, here you are. What in the world is to be done? Your aunt's locked up in her bedroom, and nobody can find the key!"

"Is that all?" answered Austin calmly. "Then she'll have to stay there till it turns up, evidently."

"But the mistress says she's sure you know all about it," panted Martha, in great distress, "and she's in a most terrible taking. Now, Master Austin, I do beseech you—'tain't no laughing matter, for the omnibus starts in a few minutes, and your aunt——"

A terrific banging was now heard from the locked-up room, accompanied by shouts and cries from the imprisoned lady. Austin advanced to the foot of the staircase, looking rather white, and listened.

"Austin! Austin! Where are you? What have you done with the key?" shrieked Aunt Charlotte, in a tempest of despair and rage. "Let me out, I say, let me out at once! It's you who have done this, I know it is. Open the door, or I shall lose the train!" A fresh bombardment from the lady's fists here followed. "Where *is* Austin, Martha? Can't you find him anywhere?"

"He's here, ma'am," cried back Martha, in quavering tones, "but he don't seem as if——"

"Call Lubin with a ladder!" interrupted the desperate lady. "I must catch the omnibus, if I break all my bones in getting out of the window. Where's Lubin? Isn't there a ladder tall enough? Austin! Austin! Where *is* Austin, and why doesn't he open the door?"

"He was here not a moment ago," replied Martha, tremulously, "but where he's got to now, or where he's put the key, the Lord only knows. Perhaps he's gone to see about a ladder. Lubin! have you seen Master Austin anywhere?"

But Austin, unobserved in the confusion, having stealthily

glanced at his watch, had slipped out at the garden gate, and now stood looking down the road. The omnibus had just started, and for about thirty seconds he remained watching it as it lumbered and clattered along in a cloud of dust until it was lost to view. Then he went back to the house, and handed the key to Martha. "There's the key," he said. "Tell Aunt Charlotte I'm going for a walk, and I'll let her know all about it when I come back to lunch."

He was out of the house in a twinkling, stumping along as hard as he could go until he reached the moors. He had played a daring game, but felt quite satisfied with the result so far, as he knew that there were no cabs to be had in the village, and that, even if his aunt were mad enough to brave a two-mile tramp along the broiling road, she could not possibly reach the station in time to catch the train. Now that the deed was done, a sensation of fatigue stole over him, and with a sigh of relief he flung himself down on the soft tussocks of purple heather, and covered his eyes with his straw hat. For half-an-hour he lay there motionless and deep in thought. No suspicion that he had acted wrongly disturbed him for a moment. Of course it was a pity that poor Aunt Charlotte should have been disappointed, and certainly that locking of her up in her bedroom had been a very painful duty; but if it was necessary—as it was—what else could he have done? No doubt she would forgive him when she understood his reasons; and, after all, it was really her own fault for having been so obstinate.

It was now half-past ten, and Austin had no intention of getting home before it was time for lunch. He had thus the whole morning before him, and he spent it rambling about the moors, struggling up hills, revelling in the heat tempered by cool grass, and wondering how Daphnis would have behaved if he had had an unreasonable old aunt to take care of; for Aunt Charlotte was really a great responsibility, and dreadfully difficult to manage. Then, coming on a deep, clear rivulet which ran between two meadows, he yielded to a sudden impulse, and, stripping himself to the skin, plunged into it, wooden leg and all. There he floated luxuriously for a while, the sun blazing fiercely overhead, and the cool waters playing over his white body. When he emerged, covered with sparkling drops, he remembered that he had no towel; so there was nothing to be done but to stagger about and disport himself like a naked faun among the buttercups and bulrushes, until the sun had dried him. As soon as he was dressed, he looked at his watch, and found that it was nearly twelve. Then he consulted a little timetable, and made a rapid calculation. It would take him just half an hour to reach the station from where he was, and therefore it was high time to start.

Off he set, and arrived there, as it seemed, at a moment of great excitement. The station-master was on the platform, in the act of posting up a telegram, around which a number of people—travellers, porters, and errandboys—were crowding eagerly. Austin joined the group, and read the message carefully and deliberately twice through. He asked no questions, but listened to the remarks he heard around him. Then he passed rapidly through the booking-office, and struck out on his way home.

Meantime Aunt Charlotte had passed the hours fuming. To her, Austin's extraordinary behaviour was absolutely unaccountable, except on the hypothesis that he was not responsible for his actions. Her rage was beyond control. That the boy should have had the unheard-of audacity to lock her up in her own bedroom in order to gratify some mad whim, and so have upset her plans for the entire day, was an outrage impossible to forgive. If he was not out of his mind he ought to be, for there was no other excuse for him that she could think of. What *was* to be done with such a boy? He was too old to be whipped, too young to be sent to college, too delicate to be placed under restraint. But she would let him feel the full force of her indignation when he returned. He should apologise, he should eat his fill of humble pie, he should beg for mercy on his knees. She had put up with a good deal, but this last escapade was not to be overlooked. Even Martha, when she came in to lay the cloth for lunch, could think of nothing to say in extenuation of his offence.

It was certainly two hours before her excitement allowed her to sit down and begin to knit. Even then—and naturally enough—while she was musing the fire burned. It never occurred to her to reflect that there must have been some *reason* for Austin's extraordinary prank, and that the first thing to be done was to discover what that was. She was too angry to take this obvious fact into consideration, and so, when Austin at last appeared, his eyes full of suppressed excitement and his forehead bathed in sweat, her pent-up wrath found vent and she flamed out at him in a rage.

For some minutes Austin stood quite silent while she stormed. If it made her feel better to storm, well, let her do it. Half a dozen times she demanded what he meant by his behaviour, and how he dared, and whether he had suddenly gone crazy, and then went on storming without waiting for his reply. Once, when he opened his mouth to speak, she sharply told him to shut it again.

It was clear, even to Martha, that if Austin's conduct had been inexplicable, his aunt's was utterly absurd.

"You've asked me several times what made me lock you up this morning," he said at last, when she paused for breath, "and each time you've refused to let me answer you. That's not very reasonable, you know. Now I've got something to tell you, but if you want to do any more raving please do it at once and get it over, and then I'll have my turn."

"Will you go to your room this instant and stay there?" cried Aunt Charlotte, pointing to the door.

"Certainly not," replied Austin. "And now I'll ask you to listen to me for a minute, for you must be tired with all that shouting." Aunt Charlotte took up her work with trembling hands, ostentatiously pretending that Austin was no longer in the room. "You wanted to go to town by the 10:27 train, and I took forcible measures to prevent you. It may therefore interest you to know what became of that train, and what you have escaped. There's been a frightful collision. The down express ran into it at the curve just beyond the signal station at Colebridge Junction, owing to some mistake of the signalman, I believe. Anyhow, in the train you wanted to go by there were five people killed outright, and fourteen others crunched up and mangled in a most inartistic style. And if I hadn't locked you up as I did you'd probably be in the County Hospital at this moment in an exceedingly unpleasant predicament."

Dead silence. Then, "The Lord preserve us!" ejaculated Martha, who stood by, in awestruck tones. Aunt Charlotte slowly raised her eyes from her knitting, and fixed them on Austin's face. "A collision!" she exclaimed. "Why, what do you know about it?"

"I called at the station and read the telegram myself. There was a crowd of people on the platform all discussing it," returned Austin, briefly.

"Your life has been saved by a miracle, ma'am, and it's Master Austin as you've got to thank for it," cried Martha, her eyes full of tears, "though how it came about, the good Lord only knows," she added, turning as though for enlightenment to the boy himself.

Then Aunt Charlotte sank back in her chair, looking very white. "I don't understand it, Austin," she said tremulously. "It's terrible to think of such a catastrophe, and all those poor creatures being killed—and it's most providential, of course, that—that—I was kept from going. But all that doesn't explain what share *you* had in it. You don't expect me to believe that you knew what was going to happen and kept me at home on purpose? The very idea is ridiculous. It was a coincidence, of course, though a most remarkable one, I must admit. A collision! Thank God for all His mercies!"

"If it was only a coincidence I don't exactly see what there is to thank God for," remarked Austin, very drily.

"'Twarn't no coincidence," averred old Martha, solemnly. "On that I'll stake my soul."

"What was it, then?" retorted Aunt Charlotte. "Anyhow, Austin, there seems no doubt that, under God, it was what you did that saved my life today. But what made you do it? How could you possibly tell that you were preventing me from getting killed?"

"I should have told you all that long ago if you weren't so hopelessly illogical, auntie," he replied. "But you never can see the connection between cause and effect. That was the reason I couldn't explain why I didn't want you to go, even before I locked you up. It wouldn't have been any use. You'd have simply laughed in my face, and have gone to London all the same."

"I don't know what you mean. Don't beat about the bush, Austin, and worry my head with all this vague talk about cause and effect and such like. What has my being illogical got to do with it?"

"Well—if you want me to explain, of course I'll do so; but I don't suppose it'll make any difference," said Austin. "Some time ago, I told you that just as I was going to get over a stile, I felt something push me back, and so I came home another way. You'll recollect that if I *had* got over that stile I should have come across a rabid dog where there was no possibility of escape, and no doubt have got frightfully bitten. But when I told you how I was prevented, you scoffed at the whole story, and said that I was superstitious.—Stop a minute! I haven't finished yet.—Then, only the other day, my life was saved from all those bricks tumbling on me when I was asleep by just the same sort of interposition. Again you jeered at me, and when I told you I had heard raps in the wall you ridiculed the idea, and—do you remember?—the words were scarcely out of your mouth when you heard the raps yourself, and then you got nearly beside yourself with fright and anger, and said it was the devil. And now for the third time the same sort of thing has happened. What is the good of telling you about it? You'd only scoff and jeer as you did before, although on this occasion it is your own life that has been saved, not mine."

Certainly Master Austin was having his revenge on Aunt Charlotte for the torrent of abuse she had poured upon him a few minutes previously. For a short time she sat quite still, the picture of perplexity and irritation. The facts as Austin stated them were incontrovertible, and yet—probably because she lacked the instinct of causality—she could not accept his explanation of them. There are some people in the world who are constituted like this. They create a mental atmosphere around them which is as impenetrable to conviction in certain matters as a brick wall is to a parched pea. They will fall back on any loophole of a theory, however imbecile and far-fetched, rather than accept some simple and self-evident solution that they start out by regarding as impossible. And Aunt Charlotte was a very apposite specimen of the class.

"I'll not scoff, at anyrate, Austin," she said at last. "I cannot forget—and I never will forget—that it's to you I owe it that I am sitting here this moment. Tell me what moved you to act as you did this morning. I may not share your belief, but I will not ridicule it. Of that you may rest assured."

"It is all simple enough," he said. "I had a horrid dream just before I woke—nothing circumstantial, but a general sense of the most awful confusion, and disaster, and terror. I fancy it was that that woke me. And as I was opening my eyes, a voice said to me quite distinctly, as distinctly as I am speaking now, '*Keep auntie at home this morning.*' The words dinned themselves into my ears all the time I was dressing, and then I acted upon them as you know. But what would have been the good of telling you? None whatever. So I tried persuasion, and when that failed I simply locked you in."

Now there are two sorts of superstition, each of which is the very antithesis of the other. The victim of one believes all kinds of absurdities blindfold, oblivious of evidence or causality. The upsetting of a salt-cellar or the fall of a mirror is to him a harbinger of disaster, entirely irrespective of any possible connection between the cause and the effect. A bit of stalk floating on his tea presages an unlooked-for visitor, and the guttering of a candle is a sign of impending death. All this he believes firmly, and acts upon, although he would candidly acknowledge his inability to explain the principle supposed to underlie the sequence between the omen and its fulfilment. It is the irrationality of the belief that constitutes its superstitious character, the contented acquiescence in some inconceivable and impossible law, whether physical or metaphysical, in virtue of which the predicted event is expected to follow the wholly unrelated augury. The other sort of superstition is that of which, as we have seen, Aunt Charlotte was an exemplification. Here, again, there is a splendid disregard of evidence, testimony, and causal laws. But it takes the form of scepticism, and a scepticism so blindly partial as to sink into the most abject credulity. The wildest sophistries are dragged in to account for an unfamiliar happening, and scientific students are accused, now of idiocy, now of fraud, rather than the fact should be confessed that our knowledge of the universe is limited. If Aunt Charlotte, for instance, had seen a table rise into the air of itself in broad daylight she would have said, "I certainly saw it happen, and as an honest woman I can't deny it; but I don't believe it for all that." The succession of abnormal occurrences, however, of which Austin had been the subject, had begun to undermine her dogmatism; and this last event, the interposition of something, she knew not what, to save her from a horrible accident, appealed to her very strongly. There was a pathos, too, about the part played in it by Austin which touched her to the quick, and she reproached herself keenly for the injustice with which she had treated him in her unreasoning anger.

She felt a great lump come in her throat as he ceased speaking, and for a moment or two found it impossible to answer. "A voice!" she uttered at last. "What sort of a voice, Austin?"

"It sounded like a woman's," he replied.

Chapter the Ninth

From this time forward Austin seemed to live a double life. Perhaps it would be more accurate to say that he inhabited two worlds. Around him the flowers bloomed in the garden, Lubin worked and whistled, Aunt Charlotte bustled about her duties, and everything went on as usual. But beyond and behind all this there was something else. The dreams and reveries that had hitherto invaded him became felt realities; he no longer had any doubt that he was encircled by beings whom he could not see, but who were none the less actual for that. And the curious feature of the case was that it all seemed perfectly natural to him, and so far from feeling frightened, or suffering from any sense of being haunted, he experienced a sort of pleasure in it, a grateful consciousness of friendly though unseen companionship that heightened his joy in life. Who these invisible guardians could be, of course he had no idea; it was enough for him just then to know that they were there, and that, by their timely intervention on no fewer than three ocasions, they had given ample proof that they both loved and trusted him.

Aunt Charlotte, on her side, could not but acknowledge that there must be "something in it," as she said; it could not all be nothing but Austin's fancy. She remembered that people who wrote hymns and poems talked sometimes of guardian angels, and it was possible that a belief in guardian angels might be orthodox. It was even conceivable that it was a benevolent functionary of this class who had let St Peter out of prison; and if the institution had existed then, why, there was nothing unreasonable in the conclusion that it might possibly exist now. She revolved these questionings in her mind during her journey up to town the day after Austin's escapade, when, as she told herself, she would be perfectly safe from accident; for it was not in the nature of things that two collisions should happen so close together. And she had reason to be glad she went, seeing that her bankers received her with perfect cordiality, and convinced her that she would certainly lose all her money if she insisted on investing it in any such wildcat scheme as the one she had set her heart upon. They suggested, instead, certain foreign bonds on which she would receive a perfectly safe four-and-a-half per cent.; and so pleased was she at having been preserved from risking her two thousand pounds that she not only indulged in a modest half bottle of Beaune with her lunch, but bought a pretty pencilcase for Austin. She determined at the same time to let the vicar know what her bankers had said about the investment he had urged upon her, and promised herself that she would take the opportunity—of course without mentioning names—of consulting him about the orthodoxy of guardian angels. He might be expected to prove a safer guide in such a matter as that than in questions of high finance.

A few days afterwards, Austin went to call upon his friend St Aubyn. He longed to see the beautiful gardens at the Court again, now that he had obtained a glimpse into the mystic side of garden-craft through the writings of Sir Thomas Browne; he felt intensely curious to pay another visit to the haunted Banqueting Hall, which had a special fascination for him since his own abnormal experiences; and he felt that a confidential talk with Mr St Aubyn himself would do him no end of good. *There* was a man, at anyrate, to whom he could open his heart; a man of high culture, wide sympathies, and great knowledge of life. He was shown into the big, dim drawing-room, where a faint perfume of lavender seemed to hang about, imparting to him a sense of quiet and repose that was very soothing; through the half closed shutters the colours of the garden again gleamed brilliantly in the sunshine, and there was heard a faint liquid sound, as of the plashing of an adjacent fountain. St Aubyn entered in a few minutes, and greeted him very cordially.

"Well, and what have you been about?" he said, after a few preliminaries had been exchanged. "Reading and dreaming, I suppose, as usual?"

"I'm afraid I've done both, and very little else to speak of," replied Austin, laughing. "I'm always reading, off and on, without much system, you know. But if I'm rather desultory I always enjoy reading, because books give me so many new ideas, and it's delightful to have always something fresh to think about."

"Yes, yes," rejoined St Aubyn. "I don't know what you read, of course, but it's clear you don't read many novels."

"Novels!" exclaimed Austin scornfully. "How *can* people read novels, when there are so many other books in the world?"

"Well, what have you been reading, then?" enquired St Aubyn, lighting a cigarette.

"I've been dipping into one of the most puzzling, fascinating, bothering books I ever came across," replied Austin, following his example. "I mean 'The Garden of Cyrus,' by Sir Thomas Browne. I can't follow him a bit, and yet, somehow, he drags me along with him. All that about the quincunx is most baffling. He seems to begin with the arrangement of a garden, and then to lead one on through a maze of arithmetical progressions till one finds oneself landed in a mystical philosophy of life and creation, and I don't know what all. If I could only understand him better I should probably enjoy him more."

St Aubyn smiled. "Well, of course, it all sounds very fanciful," he said. "One must read him as one reads all those curious old mediæval authors, who are full of pseudo-science and theories based on fables. His great charm to me is his style, which is singularly rich and chaste. But I've no doubt whatever, myself, that a great deal of this ancient lore, which we have been accustomed to regard as so much sciolism, not to say pure nonsense, had a germ of truth in it, and that truth I believe we are gradually beginning to rediscover. You see, one mustn't always take the formulas employed by these old writers in their literal sense. Many were purely symbolic, and concealed occult meanings. Now the philosopher's stone, to take a familiar example, was not a stone at all. The word was no more than a symbol, and covered a search for one of the great secrets—the origin of life, or the nature of matter, or the attainment of immortality. They seem to us to have taken a very roundabout route in their investigations, but their object was often very much the same as that of every chemist and biologist of the present day. Take alchemy, again, which is supposed by people generally to have been nothing but an attempt to turn the baser metals into gold. According to the Rosicrucians, who may be supposed to have known something about it, alchemy was the science of guiding the invisible processes of life for the purpose of attaining certain results in both the physical and spiritual spheres. Chemistry deals with inanimate substances, alchemy with the principle of life itself. The highest aim of the alchemist was the evolution of a divine and immortal being out of a mortal and semi-animal man; the development, in short, of all those hidden properties which lie latent in man's nature."

"That is a very valuable thing to know," observed Austin, greatly interested. "Every day I live, the more I realise the truth that everything we see is on the surface, and that there's a whole world of machinery—I can't think of a better term—working at the back of it. It's like a clock. The face and the hands are all we see, but it's the works inside that we can't see that make it go."

"Excellently put," returned St Aubyn. "There are influences and forces all round us of which we only notice the effects, and how far these forces are intelligent is a very curious question. I see nothing unscientific myself in the hypothesis that they may be."

"I wonder!" exclaimed Austin. "Do you know—I have had some very funny experiences myself lately, that can't be explained on any other ground that I can think of. The first occurred the very day that I was here first. Would you mind if I told you about them? Would it bother you very much?"

"On the contrary! I shall listen with the greatest interest, I assure you," replied St Aubyn, with a smile.

So Austin began at the beginning, and gave his friend a clear, full, circumstantial account of the three occurrences which had made so deep an impression on his mind. The story of the bricks riveted the attention of his hearer, who questioned him closely about a number of significant details; then he went on to the incident of Aunt Charlotte's proposed journey, the mysterious warning he had received, and the desperate measures to which he had been driven to keep her from going out. St Aubyn shouted with laughter as Austin gravely described how he had locked her up in her bedroom, and how lustily she had banged and screamed to be released before it was too late to catch the train. The sequel seemed to astonish him, and he fell into a musing silence.

"You tell your story remarkably well," he said at last, "and I don't mind confessing that the abnormal character of the whole thing strikes me as beyond question. Any attempt to explain such sequences by the wornout old theory of imagination or coincidence would be manifestly futile. Such coincidences, like miracles, do not happen. Many things have happened that people call miracles, by which they mean a sort of divine conjuring-trick that is performed or brought about by violating or annihilating natural laws. That, of course, is absurd. Nothing happens but in virtue of natural laws, laws just as natural and inherent in the universal scheme of things as gravitation or the precession of the equinoxes, *only* outside our extremely limited knowledge of the universe. That, under certain conditions, such interpositions affecting physical organisms may be produced by invisible agencies is, in my view, eminently conceivable. It is purely a question of evidence."

"I am so glad you think so," replied Austin. "It makes things so much easier. And then it's so pleasant to think that one is really surrounded by unseen friends who are looking after one. I was never a bit afraid of ghosts, and *my* ghosts are apparently a charming set of people. I wonder who they are?"

"Ah, that is more than I can tell you," answered the other,

laughing. "I'm not so favoured as you appear to be. But come, let's have a stroll round the garden. You don't mind the sun, I know."

"And the Banqueting Hall! I insist on the Banqueting Hall," added Austin, who now began to feel quite at home with his genial host. "I long to be in there again. I'm sure it's full of wonders, if one only had eyes to see."

"By all means," smiled St Aubyn, as they went out. "You shall take your fill of them, never fear. Don't forget your hat—the sun's pretty powerful today. Doesn't the lawn look well?"

"Lovely," assented Austin, admiringly. "Like a great green velvet carpet. How do you manage to keep it in such good condition?"

"By plenty of rolling and watering. That's the only secret. Let's walk this way, down to the pool where the lilies are. There'll be plenty of shade under the trees. Do you see that old statue, just over there by the wall? That's a great favourite of mine. It always looks to me like a petrified youth, a being that will never grow old in soul although its form has existed for centuries, and the stone it's made of for thousands of thousands of years. That's an illustration of the saying that whom the gods love die young. Not that they die in youth, but that they never really grow old, let them live for eighty years or more, as we count time. They remain always young in soul, however long their bodies last. Perhaps that's what Isaiah had in his mind when he talked about a child dying at a hundred. *You'll* never grow old, you know."

"Shan't I? How nice," exclaimed Austin, brightly. "I certainly can't fancy myself old a bit. How funny it would be if one always preserved one's youthful shape and features, while one's skin got all cracked and rough and wrinkled like that old youth over there! The effect would be rather ghastly. But I don't want to grow old in any sense. I should like to remain a boy all my life. I suppose that in the other world people may live a thousand years and always remain eighteen. I'm nearly eighteen myself."

St Aubyn could not help casting a glance of keen interest at the boy as he said this. A presentiment shot through him that that might actually be the destiny of the pure-souled, enthusiastic young creature who had just uttered the suggestive words. Austin's long, pale face, slender form, and bright, far-away expression carried with them the idea that perhaps he might not stay very long where he was. A sudden pang made itself felt as the possibility occurred to him, and he rapidly changed the subject.

"I don't think I'd let my thoughts run too much on mystical questions if I were you, Austin," he said. "I mean in connection with these curious experiences you've been having. You have enough joy in life, joy from the world around you, to dispense with speculations about the unseen. All that sort of thing is premature, and if it takes too great a hold upon you its tendency will be to make you morbid."

"It hasn't done so yet," replied Austin. "As far as I can judge of the other world, it seems quite as joyous and lively as this one, and in reality I expect it's a good deal more so. I don't hanker after experiences, as you call them, but hitherto whenever they've come they've always been helpful and agreeable—never terrifying or ghastly in the very least. And I don't lay myself out for them, you know. I just feel that there *is* something near me that I can't see, and that it's pleasant and friendly. The thought is a happy one, and makes me enjoy the world I live in all the more."

"Well, then, let us enjoy it together, and talk about orchids and tulips, and things we can see and handle," said St Aubyn, cheerfully. "How's Aunt Charlotte, for instance? Has she quite forgiven you for having saved her life?"

"Oh, quite, I think," replied Austin, his eyes twinkling. "I believe she's almost grateful, for when she came back from town she presented me with a gold pencil-case. She doesn't often do that sort of thing, poor dear, and I'm sure she meant it as a sign of reconciliation. It's pretty, isn't it?" he added, taking it out of his pocket.

"Charming," assented St Aubyn. "That bit of lapis lazuli at the top, with a curious design upon it, is by way of being an amulet, I suppose?"

"H'm! I don't believe in amulets, you know," said Austin, nodding sagely. "I consider that all nonsense."

"Yet there's no doubt that some amulets have influence," remarked St Aubyn. "If a piece of amber, for example, has been highly magnetised by a 'sensitive,' as very psychic persons are called, it is quite possible that, worn next the skin, a certain amount of magnetic fluid may be transmitted to the wearer, producing a distinct effect upon his vitality. There's nothing occult about that. The most thoroughgoing materialist might acknowledge it. But when it comes to spells, and all that gibberish, there, of course, I part company. The magical power of certain precious stones may be a fact of nature, but I see no proof of its truth, and therefore I don't believe in it."

"And now may we go and look at the flowers?" suggested Austin.

"Come along," returned St Aubyn. "What a boy you are for

flowers! Do you know much of botany?"

"No—yes, a little—but not nearly as much as I ought," said Austin, as they strolled through the blaze of colour. "I love flowers for their beauty and suggestiveness, irrespective of the classifications to which they may happen to belong. A garden is to me the most beautiful thing in the world. There's something sacred about it. Everything that's beautiful is good, and if it isn't beautiful it can't be good, and when one realises beauty one is happy. That's why I feel so much happier in gardens than in church."

"Why, aren't you fond of church?" asked St Aubyn, amused.

"A garden makes me happier," said Austin. "Religion seems to encourage pain, and ugliness, and mourning. I don't know why it should, but nearly all the very religious people I know are solemn and melancholy, as though they hadn't wits enough to be anything else. They only understand what is uncomfortable, just as beasts of burden only understand threats and beatings. I suppose it's a question of culture. Now I learn more of what *I* call religion from fields, and trees, and flowers than from anything else. I don't believe that if the world had consisted of nothing but cities any real religion would ever have been evolved at all."

"Crude, my dear Austin, very crude!" remarked St Aubyn, patting his shoulder as they walked. "There's more in religion than that, a great deal. Beware of generalising too widely, and don't forget the personal equation. Now, come and have a look at the orchids. I've got one or two rather fine ones that you haven't seen."

He led the way towards the orchid-houses. Here they spent a delightful quarter of an hour, and it was only the thought of his visit to the Banqueting Hall that reconciled Austin to tearing himself away. St Aubyn seemed much diverted at his insistence, and asked him whether he expected to find the figures on the tapestry endowed with life and disporting themselves about the room for his entertainment.

"I wish they would!" laughed Austin. "What fun it would be. I'm sure they'd enjoy it too. How old is the tapestry, by the way?"

"It's fifteenth century work, I believe," replied St Aubyn. "Here we are. It really is very good of its kind, and the colours are wonderfully preserved."

"It's lovely!" sighed Austin, as he walked slowly up the hall, feasting his eyes once more on the beautiful fabrics. "What a thing to live with! Just think of having all these charming people as one's daily companions. I shouldn't want them to come to life, I like them just as they are. If they moved or spoke the charm would be broken. Why don't you spend hours every day in this wonderful place?"

"My dear boy, I haven't such an imagination as you have," answered St Aubyn, laughing. "But as a mere artist, of course I appreciate them as much as anyone, just as I appreciate statuary or pictures. And I prize them for their historical value too."

Austin made no reply. He began to look abstracted, as though listening to something else. The sun had begun to sink on the other side of the house, leaving the hall itself in comparative shadow.

"Don't you feel anything?" he said at last, in an undertone.

"Nothing whatever," replied St Aubyn. "Do you?"

"Yes. Hush! No—it was nothing. But I feel it—all round me. The most curious sensation. The room's full. Some of them are behind me. Don't you feel a wind?"

"Indeed I don't," said St Aubyn. "There's not a breath stirring anywhere."

They were standing side by side. Austin gently put out his right hand and grasped St Aubyn's left.

"*Now* don't you feel anything?" he asked.

"Yes—a sort of thrill. A tingling in my arm," replied St Aubyn. "That's rather strange. But it comes from you, not from——" He paused.

"It comes *through* me," said Austin.

They stood for a few seconds in unbroken silence. Then St Aubyn suddenly withdrew his hand. "This is unhealthy!" he said, with a touch of abruptness. "You must be highly magnetic. Your organism is 'sensitive,' and that's why you experience things that I don't."

"Oh, why did you break the spell?" cried Austin, regretfully. "What harm could it have done you? You said yourself just now that nothing happens that isn't natural. And this is natural enough, if one could only understand the way it works."

"Many things are natural that are not desirable," returned St Aubyn, walking up and down. "It's quite natural for people to go to sea, but it makes some of them seasick, nevertheless, and they had better stay on shore. It's all a matter of temperament, I suppose, and what is pleasant for you is something that my own instincts warn me very carefully to avoid."

Austin drew his handkerchief across his eyes, as though beginning to come back to the realities of life. "I daresay," he said, vaguely. "But it's very restful here. The air seems to make me sleepy. I almost think—"

At this point a servant appeared at the other end of the hall, and St Aubyn went to see what he wanted. The next moment he returned, with quickened steps.

"Come away with you—you and your spooks!" he cried, cheerfully, taking Austin by the arm. "Here's an old aunt of mine suddenly dropped from the skies, and clamouring for a cup of tea. We must go in and entertain her. She's all by herself in the library."

"I shall be very glad," said Austin. "You go on first, and I'll be with you in two minutes."

So St Aubyn strode off to welcome his elderly relative, and when Austin came into the room he found his friend stooping over a very small, very dowdy old lady dressed in rusty black silk, with a large bonnet rather on one side, who was standing on tiptoe, the better to peck at St Aubyn's cheek by way of a salute. She had small, twinkling eyes, a wrinkled face, and the very honestest wig that Austin had ever seen; and yet there was an air and a style about the old body which somehow belied her quaint appearance, and suggested the idea that she was something more than the insignificant little creature that she looked at first sight. And so in fact she was, being no less a personage than the Dowager-Countess of Merthyr Tydvil, and a very great lady indeed.

"But, my dear aunt, why did you never let me know that I might expect you?" St Aubyn was saying as Austin entered. "I might have been miles away, and you'd have had all your journey for nothing."

"My dear, I'm staying with the people at Cleeve Castle, and I thought I'd just give 'em the slip for an hour or two and take you by surprise," answered the old lady as she sat down. "No, you needn't ring—I ordered tea as soon as I came in. They just bore me out of my life, you see, and they've got a pack o' riffraff staying with 'em that I don't know how to sit in the same room with. But who's your young friend over there? Why don't you introduce him?"

"I beg your pardon!" said St Aubyn. "Mr Austin Trevor, a near neighbour of mine. Austin, my aunt, Lady Merthyr Tydvil."

"Why, of course I know now," said the old lady, nodding briskly. "So you're Austin, are you? Roger was telling me about you not three weeks ago. Well, Austin, I like the looks of you, and that's more than I can say of most people, I can tell you. How long have you been living hereabouts?"

"Ever since I can remember," Austin said.

"Roger, do touch the bell, there's a good creature," said Lady Merthyr Tydvil. "That man of yours must be growing the tea-plants, I should think. Ah, here he is. I'm gasping for something to drink. Did the water boil, Richards? You're sure? How many spoonfuls of tea did you put in? H'm! Well, never mind now. I shall be better directly. What are those? Oh—Nebuchadnezzar sandwiches. Very good. That's all we want, I think."

She dismissed the man with a gesture as though the house belonged to her, while St Aubyn looked on, amused.

"I thought I should never get here," she continued. "The driver was a perfect imbecile, my dear—didn't know the country a bit. And it's not more than seven miles, you know, if it's as much. I was sure the wretch was going wrong, and if I hadn't insisted on pulling him up and asking a respectable-looking body where the house was I believe we should have been wandering about the next shire at this moment. I've no patience with such fools."

"And how long are you staying at Cleeve?" asked St Aubyn, supplying her with sandwiches.

"I've been there nearly a week already, and the trouble lasts three days more," replied his aunt, as she munched away. "The Duke's a fool, and she's worse. Haven't the ghost of an idea, either of 'em, how to mix people, you know. And what with their horrible charades, and their nonsensical round games, and their everlasting bridge, I'm pretty well at the end of my tether. Never was among such a beef-witted set of addlepates since I was born. The only man among 'em who isn't a hopeless booby's a Socialist, and he's been twice in gaol for inciting honest folks not to pay their taxes. Oh, they're a precious lot, I promise you. I don't know what we're coming to, I'm sure."

"But it's so easy not to do things," observed St Aubyn, lazily. "Why on earth do you go there? I wouldn't, I know that."

"Why does anybody do anything?" retorted the old lady. "We can't all stay at home and write books that nobody reads, as you do."

Austin looked up enquiringly. He had no idea that St Aubyn was an author, and said so.

"What, you didn't know that Roger wrote books?" said the old lady, turning to him. "Oh yes, he does, my dear, and very fine books too—only they're miles above the comprehension of stupid old women like me. Probably you've not a notion what a learned person he really is. I don't even know the names of the things he writes of."

"And you never told me!" said Austin to his friend. "But you'll have to lend me some of your books now, you know. I'm dying to know what they're all about."

"They're chiefly about antiquities," responded St Aubyn; "early Peruvian, Mexican, Egyptian, and so on. You're perfectly welcome to read them all if you care to. They're not at all deep, whatever my aunt may say."

During this brief interchange of remarks, Lady Merthyr Tydvil had been gazing rather fixedly at Austin, with her head on one side like an enquiring old bird, and a puzzled expression on her face.

"The most curious likeness!" she exclaimed. "Now, how is it that your face seems so familiar to me, I wonder? I've certainly never seen you anywhere before, and yet—and yet—who *is* it you remind me of, for goodness' sake?"

"I wish I could tell you," replied Austin, laughing. "Likenesses are often quite accidental, and it may be——"

"Stuff and nonsense, my dear," interrupted the old lady, brusquely. "There's nothing accidental about this. You're the living image of somebody, but who it is I can't for the life of me imagine. What do you say your name is?"

"My surname, you mean?—Trevor," replied Austin, beginning to be rather interested.

"Trevor!" cried Lady Merthyr Tydvil, her voice rising almost to a squeak. "No relation to Geoffrey Trevor who was in the 16th Lancers?"

"He was my father," said Austin, much surprised.

"Why, my dear, my dear, he was a *great* friend of mine!" exclaimed the old lady, raising both her hands. "I knew him twenty years ago and more, and was fonder of him than I ever let out to anybody. Of course it doesn't matter a bit now, but I always told him that if I'd been a single woman, and a quarter of a century younger, I'd have married him out of hand. That was a standing joke between us, for I was old enough to be his mother, and he was already engaged—ah, and a sweet pretty creature she was, too, and I don't wonder he fell in love with her. So you are Geoffrey's son! I can scarcely believe it, even now. But it's your mother you take after, not Geoffrey. She was a Miss—Miss——"

"Her maiden name was Waterfield," interpolated Austin.

"So it was, so it was!" assented the old lady, eagerly. "What a memory you've got, to be sure. One of Sir Philip Waterfield's daughters, down in Leicestershire. And her other name was Dorothea. Why, I remember it all now as though it had happened yesterday. Your father made me his confidante all through; such a state as he was in you never saw, wondering whether she'd have him, never able to screw up his courage to ask her, now all down in the dumps and the next day halfway up to the moon. Well, of course they were married at last, and then I somehow lost sight of them. They went abroad, I think, and when they came back they settled in some place on the other side of nowhere and I never saw them again. And you are their son Austin!"

Interested as he was in these reminiscences, Austin could not help being struck with the wonderful grace of this curious old lady's gestures. In spite of her skimpy dress and antiquated bonnet, she was, he thought, the most exquisitely-bred old woman he had ever seen. Every movement was a charm, and he watched her, as she spoke, with growing fascination and delight.

"It is quite marvellous to think you knew my parents," he said in reply, "while I have no recollection of either of them. My mother died when I was born, and my father a year or two later. What was my mother like? Did you know her well?"

"She was a delicate-looking creature, with a pale face and dark-grey eyes," answered the old lady, "and you put me in mind of her very strongly. I didn't know her very well, but I remember your father bringing her to call on me when they were first engaged, and a wonderfully handsome couple they were. No doubt they were very happy, but their lives were cut short, as so often happens, leaving a lot of stupid people alive that the world could well dispense with. But I see you've lost one of your legs! How did that come about, I should like to know?"

"Oh—something went wrong with the bone, and it had to be cut off," said Austin, rather vaguely.

"Dear, dear, what a pity," was the old lady's comment. "And are you very sorry for yourself?"

"Not in the least," said Austin, smiling brightly. "I've got quite fond of my new one."

"You're quite a philosopher, I see," said the old lady, nodding; "as great a philosopher as the fox who couldn't reach the grapes, and he was one of the wisest who ever lived. And now I think I'll have another cup of tea, Roger, if there's any left. Give me two lumps of sugar, and just enough cream to swear by."

The conversation now became more general, and Austin, thinking that the countess would like to be alone with her nephew for a few minutes before returning to the Castle, watched for an opportunity of taking leave. He soon rose, and said he must be going home. The old lady shook hands with him in the most cordial manner, telling him that in no case must he ever forget his mother—oblivious, apparently, of the fact that by no earthly possibility could he remember her; and St Aubyn accompanied him to the door. "You've quite won her heart," he said, laughingly, as he bade the boy farewell. "If she was ever in love with your father, she seems to have transferred her affections to you. Good-bye—and don't let it be too long before you come again."

Austin brandished his leg with more than usual haughtiness as he thudded his way home along the road. He always gave it a sort of additional swing when he was excited or pleased, and on this particular occasion his gait was almost defiant. It must be confessed that, never having known either of his parents, he had not hitherto thought much about them. There was one small and much-faded photograph of his father, which Aunt Charlotte kept locked up in a drawer, but of his mother there was no likeness at all, and he had no idea whatever of her appearance. But now he began to feel more interest in them, and a sense of longing, not unmixed with curiosity, took possession of him. What sort of a woman, he wondered, could that unknown mother have been? Well, physically he was himself like her—so Lady Merthyr Tydvil had said; and so much like her that it was through that very resemblance that all these interesting discoveries had been made. Then his thoughts reverted to what Aunt Charlotte had told him about his mother's dying words, and how bitterly she had grieved at not living to bring him up herself. And yet she was still alive—somewhere—though in a world removed. Of course he couldn't remember her, having never seen her, *but she had not forgotten him*—of that he felt convinced. That was a curious reflection. His mother was alive, and mindful of him. He could not prove it, naturally, but he knew it all the same. He realised it as though by instinct. And who could tell how near she might be to him? Distance, after all, is not necessarily a matter of miles. One may be only a few inches from another person, and yet if those inches are occupied by an impenetrable wall of solid steel, the two will be as much separated as though an ocean rolled between them. On the other hand, Austin had read of cases in which two friends were actually on the opposite sides of an ocean, and yet, through some mysterious channel, were sometimes conscious, in a subconscious way, of each other's thoughts and circumstances. Perhaps his mother could even see him, although he could not see her. It was all a very fascinating puzzle, but there was some truth underlying it somewhere, if he could only find it out.

Chapter the Tenth

Austin returned in plenty of time to spend a few minutes loitering in the garden after he had dressed for dinner. It was a favourite habit of his, and he said it gave him an appetite; but the truth was that he always loved to be in the open air to the very last moment of the day, watching the colours of the sky as they changed and melted into twilight. On this particular evening the heavens were streaked with primrose, and pale iris, and delicate limpid green; and so absorbed was he in gazing at this splendour of dissolving beauty that he forgot all about his appetite, and had to be called twice over before he could drag himself away.

"Well, and did you have an interesting visit?" asked Aunt Charlotte, when dinner was halfway through. "You found Mr St Aubyn at home?"

Austin had been unusually silent up till then, being somewhat preoccupied with the experiences of the afternoon. He wanted to ask his aunt all manner of questions, but scarcely liked to do so as long as the servant was waiting. But now he could hold out no longer.

"Yes—even more interesting than I hoped," he answered. "I had plenty of delightful chat with St Aubyn, and then a visitor came in. It's that that I want to talk about."

"A visitor, eh?" said Aunt Charlotte, her attention quickening. "What sort of a visitor? A lady?"

"Yes, an old lady," replied Austin, "who——"

"Did she come in an open fly?" pursued Aunt Charlotte, helping herself to sauce.

"Why, how did you know? I believe she did," said Austin. "She had driven over from Cleeve."

"Well, then, I must have seen her," said Aunt Charlotte. "A queer-looking old person in a great bonnet. I happened to be walking through the village, and she stopped the fly to ask me the way to the Court, and I remember wondering who she could possibly be. I suppose it was she whom you met there."

"What, was it *you* she asked?" exclaimed Austin, opening his eyes. "She told us the driver didn't know the way, and that she'd enquired—oh dear, oh dear, how funny!"

"What's funny?" demanded Aunt Charlotte, abruptly.

"Oh, never mind, I can't tell you, and it doesn't matter in the least," said Austin, beginning to giggle. "Only I shouldn't have known it was you from her description."

"Why, what did she say?" Aunt Charlotte was getting suspicious.

"My dear auntie, she didn't know who you were, of course," replied Austin, "and she bore high testimony to the respectability of your appearance, that's all. Only it's so funny to think it was you. It never occurred to me for a moment."

"What did she *say*, Austin?" repeated Aunt Charlotte, sternly. "I insist upon knowing her exact words. Of course it doesn't really matter what a poor old thing like that may have said, but I always like to be precise, and it's just as well to know how one strikes a stranger. It wasn't anything rude, I hope, for I'm sure I answered her quite kindly."

The servant was out of the room. "No, auntie, I don't think it was rude, but it was so comic——"

"Do stop giggling, and tell me what it was," interrupted Aunt Charlotte, impatiently.

"Well, she only said you were a respectable-looking body," replied Austin, as gravely as he could. "And so you are, you know, auntie, though, perhaps, if I had to describe you I should put it in rather different words. I'm sure she meant it as a compliment."

"Upon my word, I feel extremely flattered!" exclaimed Aunt Charlotte, reddening. "A respectable-looking body, indeed! Well, it's something to know I look respectable. And who was this very patronising old person, pray? Some old nurse or other, I should say, to judge by her appearance."

"She was the Countess of Merthyr Tydvil, St Aubyn's aunt," said Austin, enjoying the joke.

"The Countess of Merthyr Tydvil!" echoed Aunt Charlotte, amazed.

"And she's staying with the Duke at Cleeve Castle," added Austin. "But that's not the point. Just fancy, auntie, she actually knew my father! She knew him before he was married, and they were tremendous friends. It all came out because she said I was so like somebody, and she couldn't think who it could be, and then she asked what my surname was, and so on, till we found out all about it. Wasn't it curious? Did you ever hear of her before?"

"Indeed I never knew of her existence till this moment," answered Aunt Charlotte, beginning to get interested. "Your father had any number of friends, and of course we didn't know them all. Well, it is curious, I must say. But she didn't say you were like your father, did she?"

"No—my mother," replied Austin. "She didn't know her

much, but she remembers her very well. She said she was a very lovely person, too."

"Your father was good-looking in a way," said Aunt Charlotte, falling into a reminiscent mood, "but not in the least like you. He used to go a great deal into society, and no doubt it was there he met this Lady Merthyr Tydvil, and any number of others. Did she tell you anything about him—anything, I mean, that you didn't know before?"

"No, I don't think she did, except that she was very fond of him and would like to have married him herself. But as she was married already, and he was engaged to somebody else, of course it was too late."

"What! She told you that?" cried Aunt Charlotte, scandalized. "What a shameless old hussy she must be!"

"Not a bit of it," retorted Austin. "She's a sweet old woman, and I love her very much. Besides, she only meant it in fun."

"Fun, indeed!" sniffed Aunt Charlotte, primly. "She may call me a respectable-looking body as much as she likes now. It's more than I can say for her."

"Auntie, you *are* an old goose!" exclaimed Austin, with a burst of laughter. "You never could see a joke. She called you a respectable-looking body, and you called her a queer old woman like a nurse. Now you say she's a shameless old hussy, and so, on the whole, I think you've won the match."

Aunt Charlotte relapsed into silence, and did not speak again until the dessert had been brought in. Austin helped himself to a plateful of black cherries, while his aunt toyed with a peach. At last she said, in rather a hesitating tone:

"Well, you've told me your adventures, so there's an end of that. But I've had a little adventure of my own this afternoon; though whether it would interest you to hear it——"

"Oh, do tell me!" said Austin, eagerly. "An adventure—you?"

"I'm not sure whether adventure is quite the correct expression," replied Aunt Charlotte, "and I don't quite know how to begin. You see, my dear Austin, that you are very young."

"It isn't anything improper, is it?" asked Austin, innocently.

"If you say such things as that I won't utter another word," rejoined his aunt. "I simply state the fact—that you are very young."

"And I hope I shall always remain so," Austin said.

"That being the case," resumed his aunt, impressively, "a great many things happened long before you were born."

"I've never doubted that for a moment, even in my most

sceptical moods," Austin assured her seriously.

"Well, I once knew a gentleman," continued Aunt Charlotte, "of whom I used to see a great deal. Indeed I had reasons for believing that—the gentleman—rather appreciated my—conversation. Perhaps I was a little more sprightly in those days than I am now. Anyhow, he paid me considerable attention——"

"Oh!" cried Austin, opening his eyes as wide as they would go. "Oh, auntie!"

"Of course things never went any further," said Aunt Charlotte, "though I don't know what might have happened had it not been that I gave him no encouragement whatever."

"But why didn't you? What was he like? Tell me all about him!" interrupted Austin, excitedly. "Was he a soldier, like father? I'm sure he was—a beautiful soldier in the Blues, whatever the Blues may be, with a grand uniform and clanking spurs. That's the sort of man that would have captivated you, auntie. Was he wounded? Had he a wooden leg? Oh, go on, go on! I'm dying to hear all about it."

"That he had a uniform is possible, though I never saw him wear one, and it may have been blue for anything I know; but that wouldn't imply that he was in the Blues," replied his aunt, sedately. "No; the strange thing was that he suddenly went abroad, and for five-and-twenty years I never heard of him. And now he has written me a letter."

"A letter!" cried Austin. "This *is* an adventure, and no mistake. But go on, go on."

"I never was more astounded in my life," resumed his aunt. "A letter came from him this afternoon. He recalls himself to my remembrance, and says—this is the most singular part—that he was actually staying quite close to here only a short time ago, but had no idea that I was living here. Had he known it he would most certainly have called, but as he has only just discovered it, quite accidentally, he says he shall make a point of coming down again, when he hopes he may be permitted to renew our old acquaintance."

"Now look here, auntie," said Austin, sitting bolt upright. "Let him call, by all means, and see how well you look after being deserted for five-and-twenty years; but I don't want a step-uncle, and you are not to give me one. Fancy me with an Uncle Charlotte! That wouldn't do, you know. You won't give me a step-uncle, will you? Please!"

"Don't be absurd, my dear; and do, for goodness' sake, keep that dreadful leg of yours quiet if you can. It always gives me the jumps when you go on jerking it about like that. Of course I should never dream of marrying now; but I confess I do feel a little curious to see what my old friend looks like after all these years——"

"Your old admirer, you mean," interpolated Austin. "To think of your having had a romance! You can't throw stones at Lady Merthyr Tydvil now, you know. I believe you're a regular flirt, auntie, I do indeed. This poor young man now; you say he disappeared, but *I* believe you simply drove him away in despair by your cruelty. Were you a 'cruel maid' like the young women one reads about in poetry-books? Oh, auntie, auntie, I shall never have faith in you again."

"You're a very disrespectful boy, that's what *you* are," retorted Aunt Charlotte, turning as pink as her ribbons. "The gentleman we're speaking of must be quite elderly, several years older than I am, and, for all I know, he may have a wife and half a dozen grownup children by this time. You let your tongue wag a very great deal too fast, I can tell you, Austin."

"But what's his name?" asked Austin, not in the least abashed. "We can't go on for ever referring to him as 'the gentleman,' as though there were no other gentlemen in the world, can we now?"

"His name is Ogilvie—Mr Granville Ogilvie," replied his aunt. "He belongs to a very fine old family in the north. There have been Ogilvies distinguished in many ways—in literature, in the services, and in politics. But there was always a mystery about Granville, somehow. However, I expect he'll be calling here in a few days, and then, no doubt, your curiosity will be gratified."

"Oh, I know what he'll be like," said Austin. "A lean, brown traveller, with his face tanned by tropic suns and Arctic snows to the colour of an old saddlebag. His hair, of course, prematurely grey. On his right cheek there'll be a lovely bright-blue scar, where a charming tiger scratched him just before he killed it with unerring aim. I know the sort of person exactly. And now he comes to say that he lays his battered, weatherworn old carcase at the feet of the cruel maid who spurned it when it was young and strong and beautiful. And the cruel maid, now in the full bloom of placid maternity—I mean maturity——"

"Hold your tongue or I'll pull your ears!" exclaimed Aunt Charlotte, scarlet with confusion. "You'll make me sorry I ever said anything to you on the subject. Mr Ogilvie, as far as I can judge from his letter, is a most polished gentleman. There's a quaint, old-world courtesy about him which one scarcely ever meets with at the present day. Just remember, if you please, that we're simply two old friends, who are going to meet again after having lost sight of each other for five-and-twenty years; and what there is to laugh about in that I entirely fail to see."

"Dear auntie, I won't laugh any more, I promise you," said Austin. "I'm sure he'll turn out a most courtly old personage, and perhaps he'll have an enormous fortune that he made by shaking pagoda-trees in India. How do pagodas grow on trees, I wonder? I always thought a pagoda was a sort of odalisque—isn't that right? Oh, I mean obelisk—with beautiful flounces all the way up to the top. It seems a funny way of making money, doesn't it. Where is India, by the bye? Anywhere near Peru?"

"Your ignorance is positively disgraceful, Austin," said Aunt Charlotte, with great severity. "I only hope you won't talk like that in the presence of Mr Ogilvie. I expect you're right in surmising that he's been a great traveller, for he says himself that he has led a very wandering, restless life, and he would be shocked to think I had a nephew who didn't know how to find India upon the map. There, you've had quite as many cherries as are good for you, I'm sure. Let us go and see if it's dry enough to have our coffee on the lawn, while Martha clears away."

Now although Austin was intensely tickled at the idea of Aunt Charlotte having had a love affair, and a love affair that appeared to threaten renewal, the fact was that he really felt just a little anxious. Not that he believed for a moment that she would be such a goose as to marry, at her age; that, he assured himself, was impossible. But it is often the very things we tell ourselves are impossible that we fear the most, and Austin, in spite of his curiosity to see his aunt's old flame, looked forward to his arrival with just a little apprehension. For some reason or other, he considered himself partly responsible for Aunt Charlotte. The poor lady had so many limitations, she was so hopelessly impervious to a joke, her views were so stereotyped and conventional—in a word, she was so terribly Early Victorian, that there was no knowing how she might be taken in and done for if he did not look after her a bit. But how to do it was the difficulty. Certainly he could not prevent the elderly swain from calling, and, of course, it would be only proper that he himself should be absent when the two first came together. A *tête-à-tête* between them was inevitable, and was not likely to be decisive. But, this once over, he would appear upon the scene, take stock of the aspirant, and shape his policy accordingly. What sort of a man, he wondered, could Mr Ogilvie be? He had actually passed through the town not so very long ago; but then so had hundreds of strangers, and Austin had never noticed anyone in particular—certainly no one who was in the least likely to be the gentleman in question. There was nothing to be done, meanwhile, then, but to wait and watch. Perhaps the gentleman would not want to marry Aunt Charlotte after all. Perhaps, as she herself had suggested, he had a wife and family already. Neither of them knew anything at all about him. He might be a battered old traveller, or an Anglo-Indian nabob, or a needy haunter of Continental pensions, or a convict just emerged from a term of penal servitude. He might be as rich as Midas, or as poor as a church-mouse. But on one thing Austin was determined—Aunt Charlotte must be saved from herself, if necessary. They wanted no interloper in their peaceful home. And he, Austin, would go forth into the world, wooden leg and all, rather than submit to be saddled with a step-uncle.

As for Aunt Charlotte, she, too, deemed it beyond the dreams of possibility that she would ever marry. In fact, it was only Austin's nonsense that had put so ridiculous a notion into her head. It was true that, in the years gone by, the attentions of young Granville Ogilvie had occasioned her heart a flutter. Perhaps some faint, far-off reverberation of that flutter was making itself felt in her heart now. It is so, no doubt, with many maiden ladies when they look back upon the past. But if she had ever felt a little sore at her sudden abandonment by the mercurial young man who had once touched her fancy, the tiny scratch had healed and been forgotten long ago. At the same time, although the idea of marriage after five-and-twenty years was too absurd to be dwelt on for a moment, the worthy lady could not help feeling how delightful it would be to be *asked*. Of course, that would involve the extremely painful process of refusing; and Aunt Charlotte, in spite of her rough tongue, was a merciful woman, and never willingly inflicted suffering upon anybody. Even blackbeetles, as she often told herself, were God's creatures, and Mr Ogilvie, although he had deserted her, no doubt had finer sensibilities than a blackbeetle. So she did not wish to hurt him if she could avoid it; still, a proposal of marriage at the age of forty-seven would be rather a feather in her cap, and she was too true a woman to be indifferent to that coveted decoration. But then, once more, it was quite possible that he would not propose at all.

The next morning Austin put on his straw hat, and went and sat down by the old stone fountain in the full blaze of the sun, as was his custom. Lubin was somewhere in the shrubbery, and, unaware that anyone was within hearing, was warbling lustily to himself. Austin immediately pricked up his ears, for he had had no idea that Lubin was a vocalist. Away he carolled blithely enough, in a rough but not unmusical voice, and Austin was just able to catch some of the words of the quaint old west-country ballad that he was singing.

> *"Welcome to town, Tom Dove, Tom Dove,*
> *The merriest man alive,*
> *Thy company still we love, we love,*
> *God grant thee still to thrive.*
> *And never will we, depart from thee,*
> *For better or worse, my joy!*
> *For thou shalt still, have our good will,*
> *God's blessing on my sweet boy."*

"Bravo, Lubin!" cried Austin, clapping his hands. "You do sing beautifully. And what a delightful old song! Where did you pick it up?"

"Eh, Master Austin," said Lubin, emerging from among the rhododendrons, "if I'd known you was a-listening I'd 'a faked up something from a French opera for you. Why, that's an old song as I've known ever since I was that high—'Tom of Exeter' they calls it. It's a rare favourite wi' the maids down in the parts I come from."

"Shows their good taste," said Austin. "It's awfully pretty. Who was Tom Dove, and why did he come to town?"

"Nay, I can't tell," replied Lubin. "'Tis some made-up tale, I doubt. They do say as how he was a tailor. But there is folks as'll say anything, you know."

"A tailor!" exclaimed Austin, scornfully, "That I'm sure he wasn't. But oh, Lubin, there *is* somebody coming to town in a day or two—somebody I want to find out about. Do you often go into the town?"

"Eh, well, just o' times; when there's anything to take me there," answered Lubin, vaguely. "On market-days, every now and again."

"Oh yes, I know, when you go and sell ducks," put in Austin. "Now what I want to know is this. Have you, within the last three or four weeks, seen a stranger anywhere about?"

"A stranger?" repeated Lubin. "Ay, that I certainly have. Any amount o' strangers."

"Oh well, yes, of course, how stupid of me!" exclaimed Austin, impatiently. "There must have been scores and scores. But I mean a particular stranger—a certain person in particular, if you understand me. Anybody whose appearance struck you in any way."

"Well, but what sort of a stranger?" asked Lubin. "Can't you tell me anything about him? What'd he look like, now?"

"That's just what I want to find out," replied Austin. "If I could describe him I shouldn't want you to. All I know is that he's a sort of elderly gentleman, rather more than fifty. He may be fifty-five, or getting on for sixty. Now, isn't that near enough? Oh—and I'm almost sure that he's a traveller."

"H'm," pondered Lubin, leaning on his broom reflectively. "Well, yes, I did see a sort of elderly gentleman some three or four weeks ago, standing at the bar o' the 'Coach-and-Horses.' What his age might be I couldn't exactly say, 'cause he was having a drink with his back turned to the door. But he was a traveller, that I know."

"A traveller? I wonder whether that was the one!" exclaimed Austin. "Had he a dark-brown face? Or a wooden leg? Or a scar down one of his cheeks?"

"Not as I see," answered Lubin, beginning to sweep the lawn. "But a traveller he was, because the barmaid told me so. Travelled all over the country in bonnets."

"Travelled in bonnets?" cried Austin. "What *do* you mean, Lubin? How can a man go travelling about the country in a bonnet? Had he a bonnet on when you saw him drinking in the bar?"

"Lor', Master Austin, wherever was you brought up?" exclaimed Lubin, in grave amazement at the youth's ignorance. "When a gentleman 'travels' in anything, it means he goes about getting orders for it. Now this here gentleman was agent, I take it, for some big millinery shop in London, and come down here wi' boxes an' boxes o' bonnets, an' tokes, and all sorts o' female headgear as women goes about in——"

"In short, he was a commercial traveller," said Austin, very mildly. "You see, my dear Lubin, we have been talking of different things. I wasn't thinking of a gentleman who hawks haberdashery. When I said traveller, I meant a man who goes tramping across Africa, and shoots elephants, and gets snowed up at the North Pole, and has all sorts of uncomfortable and quite incredible adventures. They always have faces as brown as an old trunk, and generally limp when they walk. That's the sort of person I'm looking out for. You haven't seen anyone like that, have you?"

"Nay—nary a one," said Lubin, shaking his head. "Would he

have been putting up at one o' the inns, now, or staying long wi' some o' the gentry?"

"I haven't the slightest idea," acknowledged Austin.

"Might as well go about looking for a ram wi' five feet," remarked Lubin. "Some things you can't find 'cause they don't exist, and other things you can't find 'cause there's too many of 'em. And as you don't know nothing about this gentleman, and wouldn't know him if you met him in the street permiscuous, I take it you'll have to wait to see what he looks like till he turns up again of his own accord. 'Tain't in reason as you can go up to every old gentleman with a brown face as you never see before an' ask him if he's ever been snowed up at the North Pole and why he hasn't got a wooden leg. He'd think, as likely as not, as you was trying to get a rise out of him. Don't you know what the name may be, neither?"

"Oh yes, I do, of course," responded Austin. "He's a Mr Ogilvie."

"Never heard of 'im," said Lubin. "Might find out at one o' the inns if any party o' that name's been staying there, but I doubt they wouldn't remember. Folks don't generally stay more'n one night, you see, just to have a look at the old marketplace and the church, and then off they go next morning and don't leave no addresses. Th' only sort as stays a day or two are the artists, and they'll stay painting here for more'n a week at a time. It may 'a been one o' them."

"I wonder!" exclaimed Austin, struck by the idea. "Perhaps he's an artist, after all; artists do travel, I know. I never thought of that. However, it doesn't matter. It's only some old friend of Aunt Charlotte's, and he's coming to call on her soon, so it isn't worth bothering about meanwhile."

He therefore dismissed the matter from his mind, and set about the far more profitable employment of fortifying himself by a morning's devotion to garden-craft, both manual and mental, against the martyrdom (as he called it) that he was to undergo that afternoon. For Aunt Charlotte had insisted on his accompanying her to tea at the vicarage, and this was a function he detested with all his heart. He never knew whom he might meet there, and always went in fear of Cobbledicks, MacTavishes, and others of the same sort. The vicar himself he did not mind so much—the vicar was not a bad little thing in his way; but Mrs Sheepshanks, with her patronising disapproval and affected airs of smartness, he couldn't endure, while the Socialistic curate was his aversion. The reason he hated the curate was partly because he always wore black knickerbockers, and partly because he was such chums with the MacTavish boys. How any self-respecting individual could put up with such savages as Jock and Sandy was a problem that Austin was wholly unable to solve, until it was suggested to him by somebody that the real attraction was neither Jock nor Sandy, but one of their screaming sisters—a Florrie, or a Lottie, or an Aggie—it really did not matter which, since they were all alike. When this once dawned upon him, Austin despised the knickerbockered curate more than ever.

On the present occasion, however, the MacTavishes were happily not there; the only other guest (for of course the curate didn't count) being a friend of the curate's, who had come to spend a few days with him in the country. The friend was a harsh-featured, swarthy young man, belonging to what may be called the muscular variety of high Ritualism; much given to a sort of aggressive slang—he had been known to refer to the bishop of his diocese as "the sporting old jester that bosses our show"—and representing militant sacerdotalism in its most blusterous and rampant form. He was also in the habit of informing people that he was "nuts" on the Athanasian Creed, and expressing the somewhat arbitrary opinion that if the Rev. John Wesley had had his deserts he would have been exhibited in a pillory and used as a target for stale eggs. There are a few such interesting youths in Holy Orders, and the curate's friend was one of them.

The party were assembled in the garden, where Mrs Sheepshanks's best tea-service was laid out. To say that the conversation was brilliant would be an exaggeration; but it was pleasant and decorous, as conversations at a vicarage ought to be. The two ladies compared notes about the weather and the parish; the curate asked Austin what he had been doing with himself lately; the friend kept silence, even from good words, while the vicar, one of the mildest of his cloth, sat blinking in furtive contemplation of the friend. Certainly it was not a very exhilarating entertainment, and Austin felt that if it went on much longer he should scream. What possible pleasure, he marvelled, could Aunt Charlotte find in such a vapid form of dissipation? Even the garden irritated him, for it was laid out in the silly Early Victorian style, with wriggling paths, and ribbon borders, and shrubs planted meaninglessly here and there about the lawn, and a dreadful piece of sham rockwork in one corner. Of course the vicar's wife thought it quite perfect, and always snubbed Austin in a very lofty way if he ever ventured to express his own views as to how a garden should be fitly ordered. Then his eye happened to fall upon the curate's friend; and he caught the curate's friend in the act of staring at him with a most offensive expression of undisguised contempt.

Now, Austin was courteous to everyone; but to anybody he disliked his politeness was simply deadly. Of course he took no notice of the young parson's tacit insolence; he only longed, as fervently as he knew how to long, for an opportunity of being polite to him. And the occasion was soon forthcoming. The conversation growing more general by degrees, a reference was made by the vicar, in passing, to a certain clergyman of profound scholarship and enlightened views, whose recently published book upon the prophet Daniel had been painfully exercising the minds of the editor and readers of the *Church Times*; and it was then that the curate's friend, without moving a muscle of his face, suddenly leaned forward and said, in a rasping voice:

"The man's an impostor and a heretic. He ought to be burned. I would gladly walk in the procession, singing the 'Te Deum,' and set fire to the faggots myself."[1]

And there was no doubt he meant it. A dead silence fell upon the party. The curate looked horribly annoyed. The ladies exclaimed "Oh!" with a little shudder of dismay. The vicar started, fidgeted, and blinked more nervously than ever. Then Austin, with the most charming manner in the world, broke the spell.

"Really!" he exclaimed, turning towards the speaker, a bright smile of interest upon his face. "That's a most delightfully original suggestion. May I ask what religion you belong to?"

"What religion!" scowled the curate's friend, astounded at the enquiry.

"Yes—it must be one I never heard of," replied Austin, sweetly. "I am so awfully ignorant, you know; I know nothing of geography, and scarcely anything about the religions of savage countries. Are you a Thug?"

"Oh, Austin!" breathed Aunt Charlotte, faintly.

"I always do make such mistakes," continued Austin, with his most engaging air; "I'm so sorry, please forgive me if I'm stupid. I forgot, of course Thugs don't burn people alive, they only strangle them. Perhaps I'm thinking of the Bosjesmans, or the Andaman Islanders, or the aborigines of New Guinea. I do get so

---

1   A fact. Said in the writer's presence by a young clergyman of the same breed as the one here described.

mixed up! But I've often thought how lovely it would be to meet a cannibal. You aren't a cannibal, are you?" he added wistfully.

"I'm a priest of the Church of England," replied the curate's friend, with crushing scorn, though his face was livid. "When you're a little older you'll probably understand all that that implies."

"Fancy!" exclaimed Austin, with an air of innocent amazement. "I've heard of the Church of England, but I quite thought you must belong to one of those curious persuasions in Africa, isn't it—or is it Borneo?—where the services consist in skinning people alive and then roasting them for dinner. It occurred to me that you might have gone there as a missionary, and that the savages had converted you instead of you converting the savages. I'm sure I beg your pardon. And have you ever set fire to a bishop?"

"Austin! Austin!" came still more faintly from Aunt Charlotte.

The vicar, scandalised at first, was now in convulsions of silent laughter. Mrs Sheepshanks's parasol was lowered in a most suspicious manner, so as completely to hide her face; while the unfortunate curate, with his head almost between his knees, was working havoc in the vicarage lawn with the point of a heavy walkingstick. The only person who seemed perfectly at his ease was Austin, and he was enjoying himself hugely. Then the vicar, feeling it incumbent upon him, as host, to say something to relieve the strain, attempted to pull himself together.

"My dear boy," he said, in rather a quavering voice, "you may be perfectly sure that our valued guest has no sympathy with any of the barbarous religions you allude to, but is a most loyal member of the Church of England; and that when he said he would like to 'burn' a brother clergyman—one of the greatest Talmudists and Hebrew scholars now alive—it was only his humorous way of intimating that he was inclined to differ from him on one or two obscure points of historical or verbal criticism which——"

"It was not," said the curate's friend.

Mrs Sheepshanks immediately turned to Aunt Charlotte, and remarked that feather boas were likely to be more than ever in fashion when the weather changed; and Aunt Charlotte said she had heard from a most authoritative source that pleated corselets were to be the rage that autumn. Both ladies then agreed that the days were certainly beginning to draw in, and asked the curate if he didn't think so too. The curate fumbled in his pocket, and offered Austin a cigarette, and Austin, noticing the unconcealed annoyance of the unfortunate young man, who was really not a bad fellow in the main, felt kindly towards him, and accepted the cigarette with effusion. The vicar relapsed into silence, making no attempt to complete his unfinished sentence; then he stole a glance at the saturnine face of the stranger, and from that moment became an almost liberal-minded theologian; He had had an object-lesson that was to last him all his life, and he never forgot it.

"Well, Austin," said Aunt Charlotte, when they were walking home, a few minutes later, "of course you *ought* to have a severe scolding for your behaviour this afternoon; but the fact is, my dear, that on this occasion I do not feel inclined to give you one. That man was perfectly horrible, and deserved everything he got. I only hope it may have done him good. I couldn't have believed such people existed at the present day. The most charitable view to take of him is that he can scarcely be in his right mind."

"What, because he wanted to burn somebody alive?" said Austin. "Oh, that was natural enough. I thought it rather an amusing idea, to tell the truth. The reason I went for him was that I caught him making faces at me when he thought I wasn't looking. I saw at once that he was a beast, so the instant he gave me an opportunity of settling accounts with him I took it. Oh, what a blessing it is to be at home again! Dear auntie, let's make a virtuous resolution. We'll neither of us go to the vicarage again as long as we both shall live."

He strolled into the garden—the good garden, with straight walks, and clipped hedges, and fair formal shape—and threw himself down upon a long chair. He had already begun to forget the incidents of the afternoon. Here was rest, and peace, and beauty. How tired he was! Why did he feel so tired? He could not tell. A deep sense of satisfaction and repose stole over him. Lubin was there, tidying up, but he did not feel any inclination to talk to Lubin or anybody else. He liked watching Lubin, however, for Lubin was part of the garden, and all his associations with him were pleasant. The scent of the flowers and the grass possessed him. The sun was far from setting, and a young crescent moon was hovering high in the heavens, looking like a silver sickle against the blue. From the distant church came the sound of bells ringing for even-song, faint as horns of elf-land, through the still air. He felt that he would like to lie there always—just resting, and drinking in the beauty of the world.

Suddenly he half rose. "Lubin!" he called out quickly, in an undertone.

"Sir," responded Lubin, turning round.

"Who was that lady looking over the garden-gate just now?"

"Lady?" repeated Lubin. "I never saw no lady. Whereabouts was she?"

"On the path of course, outside. A second ago. She stood looking at me over the gate, and then went on. Run to the gate and see how far she's got—quick!"

Lubin did as he was bidden without delay, looking up and down the road. Then he returned, and soberly picked up his broom.

"There ain't no lady there," he said. "No one in sight either way. Must 'a been your fancy, Master Austin, I expect."

"Fancy, indeed!" retorted Austin, excitedly. "You'll tell me next it's my fancy that I'm looking at you now. A lady in a large hat and a sort of light-coloured dress. She *must* be there. There's nowhere else for her to be, unless the earth has swallowed her up. I'll go and look myself."

He struggled up and staggered as fast as he could go to the gate. Then he pushed it open and went out as far as the middle of the road from which he could see at least a hundred yards each way. But not a living creature was in sight.

"It's enough to make one's hair stand on end!" he exclaimed, as he came slowly back. "Where can she have got to? She was here—here, by the gate—not twenty seconds ago, only a few yards from where I was sitting. Don't talk to me about fancy; that's sheer nonsense. I saw her as distinctly as I see you now, and I should know her again directly if I saw her a year hence. Of all inexplicable things!"

There was no more lying down. He was too much puzzled and excited to keep still. Up and down he paced, cudgelling his brains in search of an explanation, wondering what it could all mean, and longing for another glimpse of the mysterious visitor. For one brief moment he had had a full, clear view of her face, and in that moment he had been struck by her unmistakable resemblance to himself.

Chapter the Eleventh

The repairs to the ceiling in Austin's room were now finished, and it was with great satisfaction that he resumed possession of his old quarters. The mysterious events that had befallen him when he slept there last, some weeks before, recurred very vividly to his mind as he found himself once more amid the familiar surroundings, and although he heard no more raps or anything else of an abnormal nature, he felt that, whatever dangers might threaten him in the future, he would always be protected by those he thought of as his unseen friends. Aunt Charlotte, meanwhile, had taken an opportunity of consulting the vicar as to the orthodoxy of a belief in guardian angels, and the vicar had reassured her at once by referring her to the Collect for St Michael and All Angels, in which we are invited to pray that they may succour and defend us upon earth; so that there really was nothing superstitious in the conclusion that, as Austin had undoubtedly been succoured and defended in a very remarkable manner on more than one occasion, some benevolent entity from a better world might have had a hand in it. The worthy lady, of course, could not resist the temptation of informing Mr Sheepshanks of what her bankers had said about the investment he had so earnestly urged upon her, and the vicar seemed greatly surprised. He had not put any money into it himself, it was true, but was being sorely tempted by another prospectus he had just received of an enterprise for recovering the baggage which King John lost some centuries ago in the Wash. The only consideration that made him hesitate was the uncertainty whether, in view of the perishable nature of the things themselves, they would be worth very much to anybody if ever they were fished up.

"Austin," said Aunt Charlotte, two days afterwards at breakfast, "I have had another letter from Mr Ogilvie. Of course I wrote to him when I heard first, saying how pleased I should be to see him whenever he was in the neighbourhood again; and now I have his reply. He proposes to call here tomorrow afternoon, and have a cup of tea with us."

"So the fateful day has come at last," remarked Austin. "Very well, auntie, I'll make myself scarce while you're talking over old times together, but I insist on coming in before he goes, remember. I'm awfully curious to see what he's like. Do you think he wears a wig?"

"I really haven't thought about it," replied his aunt. "It's nothing to me whether he does or not—or to you either, for the matter of that. Of course you must present yourself to him some time or other; it would be most discourteous not to. And do, if you can, try and behave rather more like other people. Don't parade your terrible ignorance of geography, for instance, as you do sometimes. He would think that I had neglected your education disgracefully, and seeing what a traveller he's been himself—"

"All right, auntie, I won't give you away," Austin assured her. "You'd better tell him what a horrid dunce I am before I come in, and then he won't be so surprised if I do put my foot in it. After all, we're not sure that he's been a traveller. He may be a painter. Lubin says that lots of painters come down here sometimes. My own idea is that he'll turn out to be nothing but a bank manager, or perhaps a stockbroker. I expect he's rolling in money."

Austin had said nothing to his aunt about the lady who had looked over the gate for one brief moment and then so unaccountably disappeared. What would have been the use? He felt baffled and perplexed, but it was not likely that Aunt Charlotte would be able to throw any light upon the mystery. She would probably say that he had been dreaming, or that he only imagined it, or that it was an old gipsy woman, or one of the MacTavish girls playing a trick, or something equally fatuous and absurd. But the more he thought of it the more he was convinced of the reality of the whole thing, and of the existence of some great marvel. That he had seen the lady was beyond question. That she had vanished the next moment was also beyond question. That she had hidden behind a tree or gone crouching in a ditch was inconceivable, to say the least of it; so fair and gracious a person would scarcely descend to such undignified manoeuvres, worthy only of a hoydenish peasant girl. And yet, what could possibly have become of her? The enigma was quite unsolvable.

The next morning brought with it a surprise. Aunt Charlotte had some very important documents that she wanted to deposit with her bankers—so important, indeed, that she did not like to entrust them to the post; so Austin, half in jest, proposed that he should go to town himself by an early train, and leave them at the bank in person. To his no small astonishment, Aunt Charlotte took him at his word, though not without some misgivings; instructed him to send her a telegram as soon as ever the papers were in safe custody, and assured him that she would not have a moment's peace until she got it. Austin, much excited at the prospect of a change, packed the documents away in the pistol-pocket of his trousers, and started off immediately after breakfast in high spirits. The journey was a great delight to him, as he had not travelled by railway for nearly a couple of years, and he derived immense amusement from watching his fellow-passengers and listening to their conversation. There was a party of very serious-minded American tourists, with an accent reverberant enough to have cracked the windows of the carriage had they not, luckily, been open; and from the talk of these good people he learnt that they came from a place called New Jerusalem, that they intended to do London in two days, and that they answered to the names of Mr Thwing, Mr Moment, and Mr and Mrs Skull. The gentlemen were arrayed in shiny broadcloth, with narrow black ties, tied in a careless bow; the lady wore long curls all down her back and a brown alpaca gown; and they all seemed under the impression that the most important sights which awaited them were the Metropolitan Tabernacle and some tunnel under the Thames. The only other passenger was a rather smart-looking gentleman with a flower in his buttonhole, who made himself very pleasant; engaged Austin in conversation, gave him hints as to how best to enjoy himself in London, asked him a number of questions about where he lived and how he spent his time, and finished up by inviting him to lunch. But Austin, never having seen the man before, declined; and no amount of persuasion availed to make him alter his decision.

On arrival in London, he got into an omnibus—not daring to call a cab, lest he should pay the cabman a great deal too much or a great deal too little—and in a short time was set down near Waterloo Place, where the bank was situated. His first care was to relieve himself of the precious documents, and this he did at once; but he thought the clerk looked at him in a disagreeably sharp and suspicious manner, and wondered whether it was possible he might be accused of forgery and given in charge to a policeman. The papers consisted of some dividend-warrants payable to bearer, and an endorsed cheque, and the clerk examined them with a most formidable and inquisitorial frown. Then he asked Austin what his name was, and where he lived; and Austin blushed and stammered to such an extent and made such confused replies that the clerk looked more suspiciously at him than ever, and Austin had it on the tip of his tongue to assure him that he really had not stolen the documents, or forged Aunt Charlotte's name, or infringed the laws in any way whatever that he could think of. But just then the clerk, who had been holding a muttered consultation with another gentleman of equally threatening aspect, turned to him again with a less aggressive expression, as much as to say that he'd let him off this time if he promised never to do it any more, and intimated, with a sort of grudging nod, that he was free to go if he liked. Which Austin, much relieved, forthwith proceeded to do.

Then he stumped off as hard as he could go to the Post Office near by, to despatch the telegram which should set Aunt Charlotte's mind at ease; and by dint of carefully observing what all the other people did managed to get hold of a telegraph-form and write his message. "Documents all safe in the Bank.—Your affectionate Austin." That would do beautifully, he thought. Then he offered it to a proud-looking young lady who lived behind a barricade of brass palings, and the young lady, having read it through (rather to his indignation) and rapidly counted the words, gave him a couple of stamps. But he explained, with great politeness, that he did not wish it to go by post, as it was most important that it should reach its destination before lunchtime; whereupon the young lady burst into a hearty laugh, and asked him how soon he was going back to school. Austin coloured furiously, rectified his mistake, and bolted.

In Piccadilly Circus his attention was immediately attracted by a number of stout, florid, elderly ladies who were selling some most lovely bouquets for the buttonhole. This was a temptation impossible to resist, and he lost no time in choosing one. It cost fourpence, and Austin was so charmed at the skilful way in which the florid lady he had patronised pinned it into the lapel of his jacket that he raised his hat to her on parting with as much ceremony as though she had been a duchess at the very least. Then, observing that his shoe was dusty, he submitted it to a merry-looking shoeblack, who not only cleaned it and creamed it to perfection but polished up his wooden leg as well; Austin, in his usual absent-minded way, humming to himself the while. During the operation there suddenly rushed up a drove of very ungainly-looking objects, who, in point of fact, were persons lately arrived from Lancashire to play a football match at the Alexandra Palace—though Austin, of course, could not be expected to know that; and two of these, staring at him as though he were a wild animal that they had never seen before, enquired with much solicitude how his mother was, and whether he was having a happy day. Austin took no more notice of them than if they had been flies, but as soon as the shoeblack had finished, and been generously rewarded, he presented them each with a penny.

"Wot's this for?" growled the foremost. "We ain't beggars, we ain't. Wot d'ye mean by it?"

"Aren't you? I thought you were," said Austin. "However, you can keep the pennies. They will buy you bread, you know."

The fellows edged off, muttering resentfully, and Austin prepared to cross the road to Piccadilly. The next moment he received a violent blow on the shoulder from an advancing horse, and was knocked clean off his legs. He was in the act of half consciously taking off his hat and begging the horse's pardon when a stout policeman, coming to the rescue, lifted him bodily up in one arm, and, carrying him over the crossing, deposited him safely on the pavement. He recovered his breath in a minute or two, and then began to walk down Piccadilly towards the Park.

The streets were gay and crowded, partly with black and grey people who seemed to be going about some business or other, but starred beautifully here and there with bright-eyed, clear-skinned, slender youths in straw hats, something like Austin himself, enjoying their release from school. Phalanxes of smartly-dressed ladies impeded the traffic outside the windows of all the millinery shops, omnibuses rattled up and down in a never-ending procession, and strident urchins with little pink newspapers under their arms yelled for all they were worth. Austin, absorbed in the cheerful spectacle, sauntered hither and thither, now attracted by the fresh verdure of the Green Park, now gazing with vivid interest at the ever-varying types of humanity that surged around him; blissfully unconscious that every one was staring at him, as though wondering who the pale-faced boy with eager eyes and a shiny black wooden leg could be, and why he went zigzagging to and fro and peering so excitedly about as though he had never seen any shops or people in his life before. At last he arrived at the Corner, and, turning into the Park, spent a quarter of an hour watching the riders in Rotten Row; then he crossed to the Marble Arch, passing a vast array of gorgeous flowers in full bloom, listened wonderingly to an untidy orator demolishing Christianity for the benefit of a little knot of errand-boys and nursemaids, took another omnibus along Oxford Street to the Circus, and, after an enchanting walk down Regent Street, entered a bright little Italian restaurant in the Quadrant, where he had a delightful lunch. This disposed of, he found that he could afford a full hour to have a look at the National Gallery without danger of losing his train, and off he plodded towards Trafalgar Square to make the most of his opportunity.

Meanwhile Aunt Charlotte received her telegram, and, greatly relieved by its contents, spent an agreeable day. It was not to be wondered at if she felt a little fluttering excitement at the prospect of seeing her old suitor, and was more than usually fastidious in the arrangement of her modest toilet. Lubin had been requisitioned to provide a special supply of the freshest and finest flowers for the drawing-room, and she had herself gone to the pastrycook's to order the cheesecakes and cream-tarts on which the expected visitor was to be regaled. Of course she kept on telling herself all the time what a foolish old woman she was, and how silly Mr Ogilvie would think her if he only knew of all her little fussy preparations; men who had knocked about the world hated to be fidgeted over and made much of, and no doubt it was quite natural they should. And then she went bustling off to impress on Martha the expediency of giving the silver tea-service an extra polish, and to be sure and see that the toast was crisp and fresh. When at last she sat down with a book in front of her in order to pass the time she found her attention wandering, and her thoughts recurring to the last occasion on which she had seen Granville Ogilvie. He had been rather a fine-looking young man in those days—tall, straight, and well set up; and well she remembered the whimsical way he had of speaking, the humorous glance of his eye, and those baffling intonations of voice that made it so difficult for her to be sure whether he were in jest or earnest. That he had confessedly been attracted by her was a matter of common knowledge. Why had she given him no encouragement? Perhaps it was because she had never understood him; because she had never been able to feel any real rapport between them, because their minds moved on different planes, and never seemed to meet. She had no sense of humour, and no insight; he was elusive, difficult to get into touch with; all she knew of him was his exterior, and that, for her, was no guide to the man beneath. Then he had dropped out of her life, and for five and twenty years she had never heard of him. Whatever chance she may have had was gone, and gone for ever. Did she regret it, now that she was able to look back upon the past so calmly? She thought not. And yet, as she meditated on those far-off days when she was young and pretty, the intervening years seemed to be annihilated, and she felt herself once more a girl of twenty-two, with a young man hovering around her, always on the verge of a proposal that she herself staved off.

She was not agitated, but she was very curious to see what he would look like, and just a little anxious lest there should be any awkwardness about their meeting. But eventually it came about in the most natural manner in the world, and if anybody had peeped into the shady drawing-room just at the time when Austin's train was steaming into the station, there would certainly have been nothing in the scene to suggest any tragedy or romance whatever. Aunt Charlotte, in a pretty white lace *fichu* set off with rose-coloured bows, was dispensing tea with hospitable smiles, while Martha handed cakes and poured a fresh supply of hot water into the teapot. Opposite, sat the long expected visitor; no lean, brown adventurer, no Indian nabob, and certainly no artist, but a tallish, large-featured, and somewhat portly gentleman, with a ruddy complexion, good teeth, and a general air of prosperity. His fashionable pale-grey frock-coat, evidently the work of a good tailor, fitted him like a glove; he wore, also, a white waistcoat, a gold eyeglass, and patent leather shoes. His appearance, in short, was that of a thoroughly well-groomed, though slightly overdressed, London man; and he impressed both Martha and Aunt Charlotte with being a very fine gentleman indeed, for his manners were simply perfect, if perhaps a little studied. He dropped his gloves into his hat with a graceful gesture as he accepted a cup of tea, and then, turning to his hostess, said——

"It is indeed delightful to meet you after all these years; it seems to bring back old times so vividly. And the years have dealt very gently with you, my dear friend. I should have known you anywhere."

It was not quite certain to Aunt Charlotte whether she could truthfully have returned the compliment. There are some elderly people in whom it is the easiest thing in the world to recognise the features of their youth. Allow for a little accentuation of facial lines, a little roughening of the skin, a little modification in the arrangement of the hair, and the face is virtually the same. Aunt Charlotte herself was one of these, but Granville Ogilvie was not. She might even have passed him in the street. That he was the man she had known was beyond question, but there was a puffiness under the eyes and a fulness about the cheeks that altered the general effect of his appearance, and in spite of his modish dress and elaborate manners he seemed to have grown just a little coarse. Still, remembering what a bird of passage he had been, and the many experiences he must have had by land and sea, all that was not to be wondered at. It was really remarkable, everything considered, that he had managed to preserve himself so well.

"Oh, I'm an old woman now," replied Aunt Charlotte with an almost youthful blush. "But I've had a peaceful life if rather a monotonous one, and I've nothing to complain of. It is very good of you to have remembered me, and I'm more glad than I can say to see you again. It's a quarter of a century since we met!"

"It seems like yesterday," Mr Ogilvie assured her. "And yet how many things have happened in the meantime! This charming house of yours is a perfect haven of rest. Why do people knock about the world as they do, when they might stay quietly at home?"

"Nay, it is rather I who should ask you that," laughed Aunt Charlotte. "It is you who have been knocking about, you know, not I. Men are so fond of adventures, while we women have to content ourselves with a very humdrum sort of life. You've been a great traveller, have you not?"

This was a mild attempt at pumping on the part of Aunt Charlotte, for Mr Ogilvie certainly did not give one the idea of an explorer. But she was consumed with curiosity to knew where he had spent the years since she had seen him last, and now brought all her artless ingenuity into play in order to find out.

"Yes, I was always a roving, restless sort of fellow," said Mr Ogilvie. "Never could stay long in the same place, you know. I often wonder how long it will be before I settle down for good."

"Well, I almost envy you," confessed Aunt Charlotte, nibbling a cheesecake. "I love travels and adventures; in books, of course, I mean. I've been reading Captain Burnaby's 'Ride to Khiva' lately, and that wonderful 'Life of Sir Richard Burton.' What marvellous nerve such men must have! To think of the disguises, for instance, they were forced to adopt, when detection would have cost them their lives! You should write your travels too, you know; I'm sure they'd be most exciting. Were you ever compelled to disguise yourself when you were travelling?"

"I should rather think so," replied Mr Ogilvie, nodding his head impressively. "And that, my dear lady, under circumstances in which disguise was absolutely imperative. The most serious results would have followed if I hadn't done so; not death, perhaps, but utter and irretrievable ruin. However, here I am, you see, safe and sound, and none the worse for it after all. What delicious cream-tarts these are, to be sure! They remind one of the Arabian Nights. In Persia, by the way, they put pepper in them."

"Oh dear! I don't think I should like that at all," exclaimed Aunt Charlotte, naïvely. "And have you really been in Persia? You must have enjoyed that very much. I suppose you saw some magnificent scenery in your wanderings?"

"Oh, magnificent, magnificent," assented the great traveller. "Mountains, forests, castles, glaciers, and everything you can think of. But I've never got quite as far as Persia, you understand, and just at present I feel more interested in England. I sometimes think that I shall never leave English shores again."

"And you are not married?" ventured the lady, with a tremor of hesitation in her voice. She had rushed on her destruction unawares.

"No—no," replied the man who had once wanted to marry her. "And at this moment I'm very glad I'm not."

"Oh, are you? Why?" exclaimed the foolish woman. "Don't you believe in marriage?"

"In the abstract—oh, yes," said Mr Ogilvie, with meaning. "But my chance of married happiness escaped me years ago."

Aunt Charlotte blushed hotly. She felt angry with herself for having given him an opening for such a remark, and annoyed with him for taking advantage of it. "Let me give you some more tea," she said.

"Thank you so much, but I never exceed two cups," replied Mr Ogilvie, who did not particularly care for tea. "And yet there comes a time, you know, when the sight of so peaceful and attractive a home as this makes one wish that one had one like it of one's own. Of course a man has his tastes, his hobbies, his ambitions—every man, I mean, of character. And I am a man of character. But indulgence in a hobby is not incompatible with the love of a fireside, and the blessings of *dulce domum*, to say nothing of the *placens uxor*, who is the only true goddess of the hearth. Yes, dear friend, I confess that I should like—that I positively long—to marry. That is why, paradoxical as it may appear, I congratulate myself on not being married already. But, of course, in all such cases, the man himself is not the only factor to be reckoned with. The lady must be found, and the lady's consent obtained. And there we have the rub."

"Dear me! how very unfortunate!" was all Aunt Charlotte could think of to remark. "And can't you find the lady?"

"I thought I had found her once," said Mr Ogilvie.

Then he deliberately rose from his chair, brushed a few crumbs from his coat, and took a few steps up and down the room. "Listen to me, dear friend," he began, in low, earnest tones. "There was a time—far be it from me to take undue advantage of these reminiscences—when you and I were thrown considerably together. At that time, that far-off, happy, and yet most tantalising time, I was bold enough to cherish certain aspirations." Here he took up his position behind a chair, resting his hands lightly on the back of it. "That those aspirations were not wholly unsuspected by you I had reason to believe. I may, of course, have been mistaken; love, or vanity if you prefer it, may blind the wisest of us. In any case, if I was vain, my pride came to the rescue, and sooner than incur the humiliation of a refusal—possibly a scornful refusal—I kept my secret locked in the inmost sanctuary of my heart, and went away." Mr Ogilvie illustrated his disappearance into vacancy by a slight but most expressive gesture of his arms. "I simply went away. And now I have come back. I have unburdened myself before you. In the years that are past, I was silent. Now I have spoken. And I am here to know what answer you have in your heart to give me."

It had actually come. She remembered how she had told herself that, though she could never dream of marrying, it really would be very pleasant to be asked. But now that the proposal had been made she felt most horribly embarrassed. What in the world was she to say to the man? She knew him not one bit better than she had done when she saw him last. He puzzled her more than ever. He did not look like a despairing lover, but a singularly plump and prosperous gentleman; and certainly the silver-grey frock-coat, and gold eyeglass, and varnished shoes struck her as singularly out of harmony with the extraordinary speech he had just delivered. Yet it was evidently impromptu, and possibly would never have been delivered at all had not she herself so blunderingly led up to it. And it was not a bad speech in its way. There was something really effective about it—or perhaps it was in the manner of its delivery. So she sat in silence, most dreadfully ill at ease, and not finding a single word wherewith to answer him.

"Charlotte," said Mr Ogilvie in a low voice, bending over her, "Charlotte."

"Mr Ogilvie!" gasped the unhappy lady, almost frightened out of her wits.

"You *once* called me Granville," he murmured, trying to take her hand.

"But I can't do it again!" cried Aunt Charlotte, shaking her head vigorously. "It wouldn't be proper. We are just two old people, you see, and—and——"

"H'm!" Mr Ogilvie straightened himself again. "It is true I am no longer in my first youth, and time has certainly left its mark upon my lineaments; but you, dear friend, are one of those whose charms intensify with years." Here he took out a white pocket-handkerchief, and passed it lightly across his eyes. "But I have startled you, and I am sorry. I have sprung upon you, suddenly and thoughtlessly, what I ought to have only hinted at. I have erred from lack of delicacy. Forgive me my impulsiveness, my ardour. I was ever a blunt man, little versed in the arts of diplomacy and *finesse*. For years I have looked forward to this moment; in my dreams, in my waking hours, in——"

"Pardon me one moment," said Aunt Charlotte, starting to her feet. "I know I'm sadly rude to interrupt you, but I hear my nephew in the hall, and I must just say a word to him before he comes in. I'll be back immediately. You will forgive me—won't you?"

She floundered to the door, leaving Mr Ogilvie no little disconcerted at his appeal being thus cut short. Austin had just come in, and was in the act of hanging up his hat when his aunt appeared.

"Well, auntie!" he said. "And has the gentleman arrived?"

"Hush!" breathed Aunt Charlotte, as she pointed a warning finger to the door. "He's in the drawing-room. Austin, you've come back in the very nick of time. Don't ask me any questions. My dear, you were right after all."

"Ah!" was all Austin said. "Well?"

"Come in with me at once, we can't keep him waiting," said Aunt Charlotte hastily. "I'll explain everything to you afterwards. Never mind your hair—you look quite nice enough. And mind—your very prettiest manners, for my sake."

What in the world she meant by this Austin couldn't imagine, but instantly took up the cue. The two entered the room together. Mr Ogilvie was standing a little distance off in an attitude of expectancy, his eyes turned towards the door. Aunt Charlotte took a step forward, and prepared to introduce her nephew. Austin suddenly paused; gazed at the visitor for one instant with an expression that no one had ever seen upon his face before; and then, falling flop upon the nearest easychair, went straightway into a paroxysm of hysterical and frantic laughter.

"Austin! Austin! Have you gone out of your mind?" cried his aunt, almost beside herself with stupefaction. "Is this your good behaviour? What in the world's the matter with the boy now?"

"It's *Mr Buskin!*" shrieked Austin, hammering his leg upon the floor in a perfect ecstasy of delight. "The step-uncle! Oh, do slap me, auntie, or I shall go on laughing till I die!"

"*Who's* Mr Buskin?" gasped his aunt, bewildered. "This is Mr Granville Ogilvie. What Buskin are you raving about, for Heaven's sake?"

"It's Mr Buskin the actor," panted Austin breathlessly, as he began to recover himself. "He was at the theatre here, some time ago. How do you do, Mr Buskin? Oh, please forgive me for being so rude. I hope you're pretty well?"

Mr Ogilvie had not budged an inch. But when Austin came in he had started violently. "Great Scott! Young Dot-and-carry-One!" he muttered, but so low that no one heard him. He now advanced a pace or two, and cleared his throat.

"I have certainly had the honour of meeting this young gentleman before," he said, in his most stately manner. "He was even kind enough to present me with his card, but I fear I did not pay as much attention to the name as it deserved. It is true, my dear lady, that I am known to Europe under the designation he ascribes to me; but to you I am what I have always been and always shall be—Granville Ogilvie, and your most humble slave."

"Is it possible?" ejaculated Aunt Charlotte faintly.

"You will, no doubt, attribute to its true source the concealment I have exercised towards you respecting my life for the last five-and-twenty years," resumed Mr Ogilvie, with a candid air. "I was ever the most modest of men, and the modesty which, from a gross and worldly point of view, has always been the most formidable obstacle in my path, prohibited my avowing to you the secret of my profession. Still, I practised no deceit; indeed, I confessed in the most artless fashion that, in my wanderings—in other words, on tour—I was compelled to assume disguises, and that some of my scenery was magnificent. But why should I defend myself? *Qui s'excuse s'accuse*; and now that this very engaging young gentleman has saved me the trouble of revealing the position in life that I am proud to occupy, there is nothing more to be said. We were interrupted, you remember, at a crisis of our conversation. I crave your permission to add, at a crisis of our lives. Far be it from me to——"

"I am afraid I am scarcely equal to renewing the conversation at the point where we broke off," said Aunt Charlotte, who now felt her wits getting more under control. "Indeed, Mr Ogilvie, I have nothing to reproach you with. I had no right to enquire what your profession was, and still less have I a right to criticise it. But of course you will understand that the subject we were speaking of must never be mentioned again."

The lover sighed. It was not a bad situation, and his long experience enabled him to make it quite effective. Silently he took his gloves out of his hat, paused, and then dropped them in again, with the very faintest and most dramatic gesture of despair. The action was trifling in the extreme, but it was performed by a play-actor who knew his business, and Aunt Charlotte felt as though cold water were running down her back. Then he turned, quite beautifully, to Austin.

"And you, young gentleman. And what have *you* to say?" he asked in a carefully choking voice.

"That I like you even better in your present part than as Sardanapalus," replied Austin, cordially.

"The tribute is two-edged," observed the actor with a shrug. And certainly he had acted well, and dressed the character to perfection. But the takings of the performance, alas, had not paid expenses. He really had a sentiment for the lady he had been wooing, and the prospect of a solid additional income—for it was clear she was in very easy circumstances—had smiled upon him not unpleasantly. And why should she not have married him? He was her equal in birth, they had been possible lovers in their youth, he had made a name for himself meanwhile, and, after all, there was no stain upon his honour. But she had now definitely refused. The little comedy had been played out. There was nothing for him to do but to make a graceful exit, and this he did in a way that brought tears to the lady's eyes. "Oh, need you go?" she urged with fatuous politeness. Austin was more friendly still; he reminded Mr Ogilvie that having returned so late he had had no opportunity of enjoying a renewal of their acquaintance, and begged him to remain a little longer for a chat and a cigarette. But Mr Ogilvie was too much of an artist to permit an anticlimax. The catastrophe had come off, and the curtain must be run down quick. So he wrenched himself away with what dignity he might, and, relapsing into his natural or Buskin phase as soon as he got outside, comforted himself with a glass of stiff whiskey and water at the refreshment bar of the railway station before getting into the train for London.

Chapter the Twelfth

As the weeks rolled on the days began perceptibly to draw in, and the leaves turned gradually from green to golden brown. It was the fall of the year, when the wind acquires an edge, and blue sky disappears behind purple clouds, and the world is reminded that ere very long all nature will be wrapped in a shroud of grey and silver. Rain fell with greater frequency, the uplands were often veiled in a damp mist, the hours of basking in noontide suns by the old stone fountain were gone, and Austin was fain to relinquish, one by one, those summer fantasies that for so many happy months had made the gladness of his life. There is always something sad about the autumn. It is associated, undeniably, with golden harvests and purple vintages, the crimson and yellow magnificence of foliage, and a few gorgeous blooms; but these, after all, are no more than indications that the glory of the year has reached its zenith, that its labours have attained fruition, and that the death of winter must be passed through before the resurrection-time of spring.

> *"Ihr Matten lebt wohl,*
> *Ihr sonnigen Waiden,*
> *Der Senne muss scheiden,*
> *Die Sommer ist bin."*

And yet the summer did not carry everything away with it. As the year ripened and decayed, other fantasies arose to take the place of those he was losing—or rather, he grew more and more under the obsession of ideas not wholly of this world, ideas and phases of consciousness that, as we have seen, had for some time past been gradually gaining an entrance into his soul. As the beauties of the material world faded, the wonders of a higher world superseded them. He still lived much in the open air, drinking in all the influences of the scenery in earth and sky, and marvelling at the loveliness of the year's decadence; but, as though in subtle sympathy with nature's phases, it seemed to him as though his own body had less vitality, and that, while his mind was as keen and vigorous as ever, he felt less and less inclined to explore his beloved, fields and woods. Aunt Charlotte looked first critically and then anxiously at his face, which appeared to her paler and thinner than before. His stump began to trouble him again, and once or twice he confessed, in a reluctant sort of way, that his back did not feel quite comfortable. Of course he thought it was very silly of his back, and was annoyed that it did not behave more sensibly. But he didn't let it trouble him over-much, for he was always very philosophical about pain. Once, when he had a toothache, somebody expressed surprise that he bore it with such stoicism, and asked him jokingly for the secret. "Oh," he replied, "I just fix my attention on my great toe, or any other part of my body, and think how nice it is that I haven't got a toothache there."

Aunt Charlotte had meanwhile grown to have much more respect for Austin than she had ever felt previously. He was now nearly eighteen, and his character and mental force had developed very rapidly of late. In spite of his inconceivable ignorance in some respects—geography, for instance—he had shown a shrewdness for which she had been totally unprepared, and a quiet persistence in matters where he felt that he was right and she was wrong that had begun to impress her very seriously. Many instances had arisen in which there had been a struggle for the mastery between them, and in every case not only had Austin had his own way but she had been compelled to acknowledge to herself that the wisdom had been on his side and not on hers. It was not so much that his reasoning powers were exceptionally acute as that he seemed to have a mysterious instinct, a sort of subconscious intuition, that never led him astray. And then there were those baffling, inexplicable premonitions that on three occasions had intervened to prevent some great disaster. The thought of these made her very pensive, and now that the vicar had set her mind at rest upon the abstract theory of invisible protectors she felt that she could harbour speculations about them without danger to her soul's welfare. That the power at work could scarcely emanate from the devil was now clear even to her, timid and narrow-minded as she was. Still, with that illogical shrinking from any tangible proof that her creed was true that is so characteristic of the orthodox, the whole thing gave her rather an uncomfortable sensation, and she would vastly have preferred to believe in spiritual or angelic ministrations as a pious opinion or casual article of faith than to have it brought home to her in the guise of knocks and raps. There are millions like her in the world today. Her religion, like everything else about her, was conventional, though not a whit the less sincere for that.

And so it came about that she felt very much more dependent upon Austin than Austin did on her, although neither of them was conscious of the fact. The chief result was that, now they had fallen into their proper positions, they got on together much better than they had done before. Austin had really accomplished something towards "educating" his aunt, as he used humorously to say, and as he represented the newer and fresher thought it was well that it should be so. I do not know that he troubled himself very much about the future. In spite of his delicate health he was full of the joy of life, and he accepted it as a matter of course that wherever his future might be spent it would be a happy and a joyous one. What was the use of worrying about a matter over which he had absolutely no control? The universe was very beautiful, and he was a part of it. And as the universe would certainly endure, so would he endure. Why, then, should he concern himself about what might be in store for him?

"You must take care of yourself, Austin," said Aunt Charlotte to him one day. "I'm afraid you've been overtaxing your strength, you know. You never would remain quiet even on the hottest days, and we've had rather a trying summer, you must remember."

"It's been a lovely summer," replied Austin, who was lying down.

"And how are you feeling, my dear?" asked Aunt Charlotte, anxiously.

"Splendid!" he assured her. "I never felt better in my life."

"But those little pains you spoke of; that weakness in your back——"

"Oh, *that!*" said Austin, slightingly. "I wasn't thinking of my body. What does one's body matter? I meant *myself*. I'm all right. I daresay my bones may be doing something silly, but really I'm not responsible for their vagaries, am I now?"

Aunt Charlotte sighed, and dropped the subject for the time being. But she was not quite easy in her mind.

One day a great joy came to Austin. He was hobbling about the garden with his aunt, when all of a sudden he saw Roger St Aubyn approaching them across the lawn. It was with immense pride that he presented his friend to Aunt Charlotte, who, as may be remembered, had been just a little huffy that St Aubyn had never called on her before; but now that he had actually come the small grievance was forgotten in a moment, and she welcomed him with charming cordiality.

"It is all the pleasanter to meet you," she said, "as I have now an opportunity of thanking you for all your kindness to Austin. He is never tired of telling me how much he has enjoyed himself with you."

"The pleasure has been divided; he certainly has given me quite as much as ever I have been fortunate enough to give him," replied St Aubyn, smiling, "What a very dear old garden you have here; I don't wonder that he's so fond of it. It seems a place one might spend one's life in without ever growing old."

"That's what I mean to do," said Austin, laughing.

"But yours is magnificent, I'm told," observed Aunt Charlotte. "A little place like this is nothing in comparison, of course. Still, you are right; we are both extremely fond of it, and have spent many happy hours in it during the years that we've lived here."

"And is that Lubin?" asked St Aubyn, noticing the young gardener a little distance off.

"Yes, that's Lubin," replied Austin, delighted that St Aubyn should have remembered him. Then Lubin looked up with a respectful smile, and bashfully touched his cap. "Lubin's awfully clever," he continued, as they sauntered out of hearing, "and *so* nice every way. He's what I call a real gentleman, and knows all sorts of curious things. It's perfectly wonderful how much more country people know than townsfolk. Of course I mean about *real* things—nature, and all that—not silly stuff you find in history-books, which is of no consequence to anybody in the world."

"Now, Austin," began Aunt Charlotte, warningly.

"Oh, you needn't be afraid," laughed St Aubyn; "Austin's heresies are no novelty to me. And a heresy, you must recollect, has always some forgotten truth at the bottom of it."

"I'm sure I hope so," replied Aunt Charlotte. "But the wind's getting a trifle chilly, and I think it's about time for tea. Austin isn't very strong just now, and mustn't run any risks."

So they went indoors and had their tea in the drawing-room, when St Aubyn let fall the information that he was starting in a few days for a short tour in Italy. It would not be long, however, before he was back, and then of course he should look forward to seeing a great deal of Austin at the Court. Then Aunt Charlotte had to promise that she would honour the Court with a visit too; whereupon Austin launched out into a most glowing and picturesque description of the orchid-houses, and the pool of waterlilies, and the tapestry in the Banqueting Hall, being extremely curious to know whether his prosaic relative would experience any of those queer sensations that had so greatly impressed himself. This suggested a reference to Lady Merthyr Tydvil, who had taken so great an interest in Austin when last he had been at the Court; and here Aunt Charlotte chimed in, being naturally anxious to hear all about the wonderful old lady who had known Austin's father so well in years gone by, and remembered his mother too. Of course St Aubyn said, as in duty bound, that he hoped the countess would have the pleasure of meeting Austin's aunt some day under his own roof, and Aunt Charlotte acknowledged the courtesy in fitting terms.

So the visit was quite a success, and Austin felt much more at his ease now that he could talk to his aunt about St Aubyn as one whom they both knew. She, on her side, was delighted with her new acquaintance, particularly as he seemed quite familiar with Austin's ethical and intellectual eccentricities, and did not seem horrified at them in the very least. The only thing that disturbed her just a little was the state of the boy's health. His spirits were as good as ever, and he seemed quite indifferent to the fact that he was not robust and hale; but there could be no doubt that he was paler and more fragile than he ought to have been, and the uneasiness he was fain to acknowledge in his hip and back worried her not a little—more, in fact, a great deal than it worried Austin himself.

The truth was that his attention was taken up with something wholly different. The allusions to his unknown mother that had been made by Lady Merthyr Tydvil, and the cropping-up of the same subject during St Aubyn's visit, had somehow connected themselves in his mind with the mysterious appearance of the strange lady at the garden gate on the evening of the tea-party at the vicarage. Lady Merthyr Tydvil had recognised a strong resemblance between his mother as she had known her and himself, and he had noticed the very same thing in the strange lady. There were the same dark eyes, the same long, pale face, even (as far as he could judge) the same shade in colour of the hair. He would have thought little or nothing of this had it not been for the inexplicable and almost miraculous vanishing of the figure when there was absolutely nowhere for it to vanish to. Austin knew nothing of such happenings; with all his reading he had never chanced to open a single book that dealt with phenomena of this class, much less any written by scientific and sober investigators, so that the entire subject was an undiscovered country to him. Had he done so, his perplexity would not have been nearly so great, and very probably he might have recognised the fact of his own remarkable psychic powers. Still, in spite of this disadvantage, the conviction was slowly but surely forcing itself upon his mind that the lady he had seen was no one but his own mother. From this to a belief that it was she who had intervened to save both himself and his Aunt Charlotte from serious disasters was but a single step; and like Mary of old, in the presence of an even greater mystery, he revolved all these things silently in his heart.

It was during the period when he was occupied with this train of thought that another strange thing occurred. One evening he strolled into the garden just as the sun was setting. It was one of those lurid sunsets peculiar to autumn, which look like a distant conflagration obscured by a veil of smoke. The western sky was aglow with a dull, murky crimson flecked by clouds of the deepest indigo, from behind which there seemed to shoot up luminous pulsations like the reflection of unseen flames. The effect of this red, throbbing light upon the garden in which he stood was almost unearthly, something resembling that of an eclipse viewed through warm-coloured glass; beautiful in itself, yet abnormal, fantastic, suggestive of weird imaginings. Austin, absorbed in contemplation, moved slowly through the shrubbery until he reached the lawn; then came to a dead stop. An astounding vision appeared before him. Standing by the old stone fountain, scarcely ten yards away, he saw the figure of a youth. The slender form was partly draped in a loose tunic of some dim, pale, reddish hue, descending halfway to his knees; on his feet were sandals of the old classic type; his golden hair was bound by a narrow fillet, and in his right hand he held a round, shallow cup, apparently of gold, towards which he was bending his head as though to drink from it. Austin stood transfixed. So exquisite a being he had never dreamt of or conceived. The contour of the limbs, the fall of the tunic, the pose of the head and throat, the ruddy lips, ever so slightly parted to meet the edge of the vessel he was in the act of raising to them, were something more than human. The whole thing stood out with stereoscopic clearness, and seemed as though self-luminous, although it shed no light on its surroundings. At that moment the youth turned his head, and met Austin's eyes with an expression that was not a smile, but something far more subtle, something that bore the same relation to a smile that a smile does to a laugh—thrilling, penetrating, indescribable. Austin flung out his hands in rapture.

"Daphnis!" he ejaculated, with a flash of intuition.

He threw himself forward impulsively, in a mad attempt to approach the wonderful phantasm. As he did so, the colours lost their sheen, and the figure faded into transparency. By the time he was near enough to touch it, it was no longer there, and the next instant he found himself clinging to the cold stone margin of the old fountain, all alone upon the lawn in the fast gathering twilight, shivering, panting, marvelling, but exultant in the consciousness of having been vouchsafed just one glimpse of the being who, so long unseen, had constituted for many years his cherished ideal of physical and spiritual beauty.

He leant upon the fountain, in the spot that the vision had occupied. "And I believe he's always been here—all these many years," mused the boy, coming gradually to himself again. "He has stood beside me, often and often, inspiring me with beautiful ideas, though I never guessed it, never suspected it for a single moment. And now he has shown himself to me at last. The fountain is haunted, haunted by the beautiful earth-spirit that has been my guide, that I've dreamt of all my life without ever having seen him. It's a sacred fountain now—like the fountains of old Hellas, sacred with the hauntings of the gods. And he actually drank of the water—or was going to, if I hadn't frightened him away. Perhaps he's still here, although I can't see him any more. I wonder whether he knows my mother. It may be that they're great friends, and keep watch over me together. How wonderful it all is!"

Then he walked slowly and rather painfully back to the house. He was in great spirits that night at dinner, though he ate no more than would have satisfied a bird, greatly to his aunt's disturbance. With much tact he abstained from saying anything to her about the extraordinary experience he had just gone through, feeling very justly that, though she seemed more or less reconciled to the ministry of angels, Daphnis was frankly a pagan spirit, and would, as such, be open to grave suspicion from the standpoint of his aunt's orthodoxy. But it didn't matter much, after all. He was happy in the consciousness that every day he was getting into nearer touch with a beautiful world that he could not see as yet, but in the existence of which he now believed as firmly as in that of his own garden. The spirit-land was fast becoming a reality to him, and although he had never beheld the glories of its scenery he had actually had a visit from two of its inhabitants. That, he thought, constituted the difference between Aunt Charlotte and himself. She believed in some place she called heaven, and had a vague notion that it was like a sort of religious transformation-scene, millions of miles away, up somewhere in the sky. He, on the contrary, knew that the spirit-world was all around him, because he had had ocular as well as intuitive demonstration of its proximity.

It must not be supposed, however, that he sank into a state of mystic contemplation that unfitted him for everyday life. On the contrary, he took more interest in his physical surroundings than ever. It was now October, and he threw himself with almost feverish energy into the garden-work belonging to that month. There were potted carnations to be removed into warmth and shelter, hyacinths and tulips for the spring bloom to be planted in different beds, roses and honeysuckles to be carefully and scientifically pruned, and dead leaves to be plucked off everywhere. His fragile health prevented him from helping in the more onerous tasks, but he followed Lubin about indefatigably, watching everything he did with eager vigilance, whether he was planting ranunculuses and anemones, or clipping hedges, or trimming evergreens; while he himself was fain to be content with pruning and budding, and directing how the plants should be most fitly set. He said he wanted the show of flowers next year to be a triumph of gardencraft. The garden was a sort of holy of holies to him, and he tended it, and planned for it, and worked in it more enthusiastically than he had ever done before. This interest in common things was gratifying to Aunt Charlotte, who distrusted and discouraged his dwelling on what she called the uncanny side of life; but she was anxious, at the same time, that he should not overtax his strength, and gave secret orders to Lubin to see that the young master did not allow his ardour to outrun the dictates of discretion.

One afternoon, Austin, who was feeling unusually tired, was lying in an easychair in the drawing-room with a book. He had been all the morning standing about in the garden, and after lunch Aunt Charlotte had put her foot down, and peremptorily forbidden him to go out any more that day. Austin had tried to get up a small rebellion, protesting that there were a lot of jonquils to be planted, and that Lubin would be sure to stick them too close together if he were not there to look after him; but his aunt was firm, and Austin was compelled on this occasion to submit. So there he lay, very calm and comfortable, while Aunt Charlotte knitted industriously, close by.

"You see, my dear, you're not strong—not nearly so strong as you ought to be," she said, as she glanced at his drawn face. "I intend to take extra care of you this winter, and if you're not good about it I shall have to call in the doctor. I feel I have a great responsibility, you know, Austin. Oh, if only your poor mother were here, and could look after you herself!"

"How do you know she doesn't?" asked Austin.

"My dear!" exclaimed Aunt Charlotte, rather shocked.

"Well, you can't be sure," retorted Austin, "and I believe

myself she does. I'm sure of one thing, anyhow—and that is that if she came into the room at this moment I should recognise her at once."

"You? Why, you never saw her in your life!" said Aunt Charlotte. "You shouldn't indulge such fancies, Austin. You could only think it might possibly be your mother, from the descriptions you've heard of her. Of course you could never be certain."

"How is it she never had her likeness taken?" enquired Austin, laying his book aside.

"She did have her likeness taken once; but she didn't care for it, and I don't think she kept any copies," replied Aunt Charlotte. "It was just a common cabinet photograph, you know, done by some man or other in a country town. There may be one or two in existence, but I've never come across any. I've often wished I could."

"There are a lot of old trunks up in the attic, full of all sorts of rubbish," suggested Austin. "It might be amusing to go up and grub about among them some day. One might find wonderful heirlooms, and jewels, and forgotten wills. I should like to hunt there awfully. I'm sure they haven't been touched for a century."

"In that case it isn't likely we should find your mother's photograph among them," retorted Aunt Charlotte briskly.

Austin laughed. "But may I?" he persisted.

"My dear, of course you may if you like," replied Aunt Charlotte. "I don't suppose there are any treasures or secrets to be unearthed; probably you'll find nothing but a lot of old bills, and schoolbooks, and such-like useless lumber. There *may* be some forgotten photographs—I couldn't swear there aren't; but if you do find anything of interest I shall be much surprised."

Austin was on his legs in a moment. "Just the thing for an afternoon like this!" he cried impulsively. "I'll go up now, and have a look round. Don't worry, auntie; I won't fatigue myself, I promise you. I only want to see if there's anything that looks as though it might be worth examining."

He hopped out of the room in some excitement, full of this new project. Aunt Charlotte, less enthusiastic, continued knitting placidly, her only anxiety being lest Austin should strain his back in leaning over the boxes. In about twenty minutes or so he returned, followed by Martha, the two carrying between them a battered green chest full of odds and ends, which she had carefully dusted before bringing into the drawing-room. "There!" he said, triumphantly; "here's treasure-trove, if you like. Put it on the chair, Martha, close by me, and then I can empty it at my leisure. Now for a plunge into the past. Isn't it going to be fun, auntie?"

"I hope, my dear, that the entertainment will come up to your expectations," observed Aunt Charlotte, equably.

"Sure to," said Austin, beginning to rummage about. "What are these? Old exercise-books, as I live! Oh, do look here; isn't this wonderful? Here's a translation: 'Horace, Liber I, Satire 5.' How brown the ink is. *Aricia a little town on the way to Appia received me coming from the magnificent city of Rome with poor accommodation. Heliodorus by far the most learned orator of the Greeks accompanied me. We came to the marketplace of Appius filled with sailors and insolent brokers.*—Were they stockbrokers, I wonder? Oh, auntie, these are exercises done by my grandfather when he was a little boy. Poor little grandfather; what pains he seems to have taken over it, and how beautifully it's written. I hope he got a lot of marks; do you think he did? *The sailor, soaked in poor wine, and the passenger, earnestly celebrate their absent mistresses.* Poor things! They don't seem to have had a very enjoyable excursion. However, I can't read it all through. Oh—here are a lot of letters. Not very interesting. All about contracts and sales, and silly things like that. Here's a funny book, though. Do look, auntie. It must have been printed centuries ago by the look of it. I wonder what it's all about. *A Sequel to the Antidote to the Miseries of Human Life, containing a Further Account of Mrs Placid and her daughter Rachel. By the Author of the Antidote.* What *does* it all mean? 'Squire Bustle'—'Miss Finakin'—'Uncle Jeremiah'—used people to read books like this when grandfather was a little boy? It looks quite charming, but I think we'll put it by for the present. What's this? Oh, a daguerreotype, I suppose—an extraordinary-looking, smirking old person in a great bonnet with large roses all round her face, and tied with huge ribbons under her chin. Dear auntie, why don't you wear bonnets like that? You *would* look so sweet! Pamphlets—tracts—oh dear, these are all dreadfully dry. What a mixture it all is, to be sure. The things seem to have been shot in anyhow. Hullo—an album. *Now* we shall see. This is evidently of much later date than the other treasures, though it is at the bottom of them all."

He dragged out an old, soiled, photographic album bound in purple morocco, and all falling to pieces. It proved to contain family portraits, none of them particularly attractive in themselves, but interesting enough to Austin. He turned over the pages one by one, slowly. Aunt Charlotte glanced curiously at them over her spectacles from where she sat.

"I don't think I remember ever seeing that album," she said. "I wonder whom it can have belonged to. Ah! I expect it must have been your father's. Yes—there's a photograph of your Uncle Ernest, when he was just of age. You never saw him, he went to Australia before you were born. Those ladies I don't know. What a string of them there are, to be sure. I suppose they were——"

"There she is!" cried Austin, suddenly bringing his hand down upon the page. "That's my mother. I told you I should know her, didn't I?"

Aunt Charlotte jumped. "The very photograph!" she exclaimed. "I had no idea there was a copy in existence. But how in the wide world did you recognise it?"

Austin continued examining it for some seconds without replying. "I don't think it quite does her justice," he said at last, thoughtfully. "The position isn't well arranged. It makes the chin too small."

"Quite true!" assented Aunt Charlotte. "It's the way she's holding her head." Then, with another start: "But how can you know that?"

"Because I saw her only the other day," said Austin.

For a moment Aunt Charlotte thought he was woolgathering. He spoke in such a perfectly calm, natural tone, that he might have been referring to someone who lived in the next street. But a glance at his face convinced her that he meant exactly what he said.

"Austin!" she exclaimed. "What can you be thinking about?"

"It's perfectly true," he assured her. "I saw her a few weeks ago in the garden. She stood and looked at me over the gate, and then suddenly disappeared."

"And you really believe it?" cried Aunt Charlotte in amaze.

"I don't believe it, I know it," he answered, laying down the photograph. "I saw her as distinctly as I see you now. It was that day we had been having tea at the vicarage, when we met the man who wanted to set fire to some bishop or other. Ask Lubin; he'll remember it fast enough."

This time Aunt Charlotte fairly collapsed. It was no longer any use flouting Austin's statements; they were too calm, too collected, to be disposed of by mere derision. There could be no doubt that he firmly believed he had seen something or somebody, and whatever might be the explanation of that belief it had enabled him not only to recognise his mother's photograph but to criticise, and criticise correctly, a certain defect in the portrait. She could not deny that what he said was true. "Can such things really be?"

she uttered under her breath.

"Dear auntie, they *are*," said Austin. "I've been conscious of it for months, and lately I've had the proof. Indeed, I've had more than one. There are people all round us, only it isn't given to everybody to see them. And it isn't really very astonishing that it should be so, when one comes to think of it."

From that day forward Aunt Charlotte watched Austin with a sense of something akin to awe. Certainly he was different from other folk. With all his love of life, his keen interest in his surroundings, and his wealth of boyish spirits, he seemed a being apart—a being who lived not only in this world but on the boundary between this world and another. As an orthodox Christian woman of course she believed in that other—"another and a better world," as she was accustomed to call it. But that that world was actually around her, hemming her in, within reach of her fingertips so to speak, that was quite a new idea. It gave her the creeps, and she strove to put it out of her head as much as possible. But ere many weeks elapsed, it was forced upon her in a very painful way, and she could no longer ignore the feeling which stole over her from time to time that not only was the boundary between the two worlds a very narrow one, but that her poor Austin would not be long before he crossed it altogether.

For there was no doubt that he was beginning to fade. He got paler and thinner by degrees, and one day she found him in a dead faint upon the floor. The slight uneasiness in his hip had increased to actual pain, and the pain had spread to his back. In an agony of apprehension she summoned the doctor, and the doctor with hollow professional cheerfulness said that that sort of thing wouldn't do at all, and that Master Austin must make up his mind to lie up a bit. And so he was put to bed, and people smiled ghastly smiles which were far more heartrending than sobs, and talked about taking him away to some beautiful warm southern climate where he would soon grow strong and well again. Austin only said that he was very comfortable where he was, and that he wouldn't think of being taken away, because he knew how dreadfully poor Aunt Charlotte suffered at sea, and travelling was a sad nuisance after all. And indeed it would have been impossible to move him, for his sufferings were occasionally very great. Sometimes he would writhe in strange agonies all night long, till they used to wonder how he would live through it; but when morning came he scarcely ever remembered anything at all, and in answer to enquiries always said that he had had a very good night indeed, thank you. Once or twice he seemed to have a dim recollection of something—some "bustle and fluff," as he expressed it—during his troubled sleep; and then he would ask anxiously whether he really had been giving them any bother, and assure them that he was so very sorry, and hoped they would forgive him for having been so stupid. At which Aunt Charlotte had to smile and joke as heroically as she knew how.

There were some days, however, when he was quite free from pain, and then he was as bright and cheerful as ever. He lay in his white bed surrounded by the books he loved, which he read intermittently; and every now and then, when Aunt Charlotte thought he was strong enough, a visitor would be admitted. Roger St Aubyn, now back from Italy, often dropped in to sit with him, and these were golden hours to Austin, who listened delightedly to his friend's absorbing descriptions of the beautiful places he had been to and the wonderful old legends that were attached to them. Then nothing would content him but that Lubin must come up occasionally and tell him how the garden was looking, and what he thought of the prospects for next summer, and answer all sorts of searching questions as to the operations in which he had been engaged since Austin had been a prisoner. Austin enjoyed these colloquies with Lubin; the very sight of him, he said, was like having a glimpse of the garden. But somehow Lubin's eyes always looked rather red and misty when he came out of the room, and it was noticed that he went about his work in a very half hearted and listless manner.

One day, however, a visitor called whose presence was not so sympathetic. This was Mr Sheepshanks, the vicar. Of course he was quite right to call—indeed it would have been an unpardonable omission had he not done so; at the same time his little furtive movements and professional air of solemnity got on Austin's nerves, and produced a sense of irritation that was certainly not conducive to his well-being. At last the point was reached to which the vicar had been gradually leading up, and he suggested that, now that it had pleased Providence to stretch Austin on a couch of pain, it was advisable that he should think about making his peace with God.

"Make my peace with God?" repeated Austin, opening his eyes. "What about? We haven't quarrelled!"

"My dear young friend, that is scarcely the way for a creature to speak of its relations with its Creator," said the vicar, gravely shocked.

"Isn't it?" said Austin. "I'm very sorry; I thought you were hinting that I had some grudge against the Creator, and that I ought to make it up. Because I haven't, not in the very least. I've had a lovely life, and I'm more obliged to Him for it than I can say."

"Ahem," coughed the vicar dubiously. "One scarcely speaks of being *obliged* to the Almighty, my dear Austin. We owe Him our everlasting gratitude for His mercies to us, and when we think how utterly unworthy the best of us are of the very least attention on His part——"

"I don't see that at all," interrupted Austin. "On the contrary, seeing that God brought us all into existence without consulting any one of us I think we have a right to expect a great deal of attention on His part. Surely He has more responsibility towards somebody He has made than that somebody has towards Him. That's only common sense, it seems to me."

The vicar thought he had never had such an unmanageable penitent to deal with since he took orders. "But how about sin?" he suggested, shifting his ground. "Have you no sense of sin?"

"I'm almost afraid not," acknowledged Austin, with well-bred concern. "Ought I to have?"

"We all ought to have," replied the vicar sternly. "We have all sinned, and come short of the glory of God."

"I don't see how we could have done otherwise," remarked Austin, who was getting rather bored. "Little people like us can't be expected to come up to a standard which I suppose implies divine perfection. I dare say I've done lots of sins, but for the life of me I've no idea what they were. I don't think I ever thought about it."

"It's time you thought about it now, then," said the vicar, getting up. "I won't worry you any more today, because I see you're tired. But I shall pray for you, and when next I come I hope you'll understand my meaning more clearly than you do at present."

"That is very kind of you," said Austin, putting out his almost transparent hand. "I'm awfully sorry to give you so much trouble. You'll see Aunt Charlotte before you go away? I know she'll expect you to go in for a cup of tea."

So the vicar escaped, almost as glad to do so as Austin was to be left in peace. And the worst of it was that, though he cudgelled his brains for many hours that night, he could not think of any sins in particular that Austin had been in the habit of committing. He was kind, he was pure, and he was unselfish. His exaggerated abuse of people he didn't like was more than half humorous, and was rather a fault than a sin. Yet he must be a sinner somehow, because everybody was. Perhaps his sin consisted in his not being pious in the evangelical sense of the word. Yet he loved goodness, and the vicar had once heard a great Roman Catholic divine say that loving goodness was the same thing as loving God. But Austin had never said that he loved God; he had only said that he was much obliged to Him. The poor vicar worried himself about all this until he fell asleep, taking refuge in the reflection that if he couldn't understand the state of Austin's soul there was always the probability that God did.

Aunt Charlotte, on her side, was too much absorbed in her anxiety and sorrow to trouble herself with such misgivings. The light of her life was burning very low, and bade fair to be extinguished altogether. What were theological conundrums to her now? It would be positively wicked to fear that anything dreadful could happen to Austin because he had forgotten his catechism and was not impressed by the vicar's prosy discourses in church. Face to face with the possibility of losing him, all her conventionality collapsed. The boy had been everything in the world to her, and now he was going elsewhere.

The house was a very mournful place just then, and the servants moved noiselessly about as though in the presence of some strange mystery. The only person in it who seemed really happy was Austin himself. A great London surgeon came to see him once, and then there was talk of hiring a trained nurse. But Austin combatted this project with all the vigour at his command, protesting that trained nurses always scented themselves with chloroform and put him in mind of a hospital; he really could not have one in the room. Some assistance, however, was necessary, for the disease was making such rapid progress that he could no longer turn himself in bed; and Austin, recognising the fact, insisted that Lubin and no other should tend him. So Lubin, tearfully overjoyed at the distinction, exchanged the garden for the sick-chamber, into which, as Austin said, he seemed to bring the very scent of grass and flowers; and there he passed his time, day after day, raising the helpless boy in his strong arms, shifting his position, anticipating his slightest wish, and even sleeping in a low truckle-bed in a corner of the room at night.

Sometimes Austin would lie, silent and motionless, for hours, with a perfectly calm and happy look upon his face. This was when the pain relaxed its grip upon him. At other times he would talk almost incessantly, apparently holding a conversation with people whom Lubin could not see. One would have thought that someone very dear to him had come to pay him a visit, and that he and this mysterious someone were deeply attached to each other, so bright and playful were the smiles that rippled upon his lips. He spoke in a low, rapid undertone, so that Lubin could only catch a word or two here and there; then there would be a pause, as though to allow for some unheard reply, to which Austin appeared to be listening intently; and then off he would go again as fast as ever. His eyes had a wistful, far-off look in them, and every now and then he seemed puzzled at Lubin's presence, not being quite able to reconcile the actual surroundings of the sick-room with those other scenes that were now dawning upon his sight, scenes in which Lubin had no place. There was a little confusion in his mind in consequence; but as the days went on things gradually became much clearer.

Now Austin, in spite of his utter indifference to, or indeed aversion from, theological religion, had always loved his Sundays. To him they were as days of heaven upon earth, and in them he appeared to take an instinctive delight, as though the very atmosphere of the day filled him with spiritual aspirations, and thoughts which belonged not to this world. Above all, he loved Sunday evenings, which appeared to him a season hallowed in some special way, when all high and pure influences were felt in their greatest intensity. And now another Sunday came round, and, as had been the case all through his illness, he felt and knew by instinct what day it was. He lay quite still, as the distant chime of the church bells was wafted through the air, faint but just audible in the silent room. Aunt Charlotte smiled tenderly at him through her tears; she was going to church, poor soul, to pray for his recovery, though knowing quite well that what she called his recovery was beyond hope. Austin shot a brilliant smile at her in return, and Aunt Charlotte rushed out of the room choking.

The day drew to its close, the darkness gathered, and Austin, who had been suffering considerably during the afternoon, was now easier. At about seven o'clock his aunt stole softly in, unable to keep away, and looked at him. His eyes were closed, and he appeared to be asleep.

"How has he been this afternoon?" she asked of Lubin in an undertone.

"Seemed to be sufferin' a bit about two hour ago, but nothing more 'n usual," said Lubin. "Then he got easier and sank asleep, quite quietlike. He's breathin' regular enough."

"He doesn't look worse—there's even a little colour in his cheeks," observed Aunt Charlotte, as she watched the sleeping boy. "He's in quite a nice, natural slumber. If nursing could only bring him round!"

"I'd nurse him all my life for that matter," replied Lubin huskily, standing on the other side of the bed.

"I know you would, Lubin," cried Aunt Charlotte. "You've been goodness itself to my poor darling. What wouldn't I do—what wouldn't we all do—to save his precious life!"

"Is he waking up?" whispered Lubin, bending over. "Nay—just turning his head a bit to one side. He's comfortable enough for the time being. If it wasn't for them crooel pains as seizes him——"

"Ah, but they're only the symptoms of the disease!" sighed Aunt Charlotte, mournfully. "And the doctor says that if they were to leave him suddenly, it—wouldn't—be a good—sign." Here she began to sob under her breath. "It might mean that his poor body was no longer capable of feeling. Well, God knows what's best for all of us. Aren't you getting nearly worn out yourself, Lubin?"

"I? Laws no, ma'am," answered Lubin almost scornfully. "I get a sort o' dog's snooze every now and again, and when Martha was here this morning I slept for four hour on end. No fear o' me caving in. Ah, would ye now?" observing some feeble attempt on Austin's part to shift his position. "There!" as he deftly slipped his hands under him, and turned him a little to one side. "That eases him a bit. It's stiff work, lying half the day with one's back in the same place."

Then Martha appeared at the door, and insisted on Aunt Charlotte going downstairs and trying to take some nourishment. In the sick-room all was silent. Austin continued sleeping peacefully, an expression of absolute contentment and happiness upon his face, while Lubin sat by the bedside watching.

But Austin did not go on sleeping all the night. There came a time when his deep unconsciousness was invaded by a very strange and wonderful sensation. He no longer felt himself lying motionless in bed, as he had been doing for so long. He seemed rather to be floating, as one might float along the current of a strong, swift stream. He felt no bed under him, though what it was that held him up he couldn't guess, and it never occurred to him to wonder. All he knew was that his pains had vanished, that his body was scarcely palpable, and that the smooth, gliding motion—if motion it could be called—was the most exquisite sensation he had ever felt. What *could* be happening? Austin, his mind now wide awake, and thoroughly on the alert, lay for some time in rapt enjoyment of this new experience. Then he opened his eyes, and found that he was in bed after all; the nightlight was burning on a table by the window, the bookcase stood where it did, and he could even discern Lubin, who seemed to have dropped asleep, in an armchair three or four yards away. That made the mystery all the greater, and Austin waited in expectant silence to see what would happen next.

Suddenly, as in a flash, the whole of his past life unrolled itself before his consciousness. He saw himself a toddling baby, a growing child, a schoolboy, a happy young rascal chasing sheep; then came a period of pain, a gradual convalescence, a joyful life in the country air, a life of reading, a life of pleasant dreams, a life into which entered his friendship with St Aubyn, his days with Lubin in the garden, his encounters with Mr Buskin, and those strange experiences that had reached him from another world. That other world was coming very near to him now, and he was coming very near to it! And all these recollections formed one marvellous panorama, one great simultaneous whole, with no appearance of succession, but just as though it had happened all at once. Austin seemed to be past reasoning; he had advanced to a stage where thinking and speculating were things gone by for ever, and his perceptions were wholly passive. There was his life, spread out in consciousness before him; and meanwhile he was undergoing a change.

He looked up, and saw a dim, violet cloud hanging horizontally over him. It was in shape like a human form; his own form. At that moment a great tremor, a sort of convulsive thrill, passed through him as he lay, jarring every nerve, and awaking him, at that supreme crisis, to the existence of his body. A sense of confusion followed; and then he seemed to pass out of his own head, and found himself poised in the air immediately over the place where he had just been lying. He saw the violet cloud no more, though whether he had coalesced with it, or the cloud itself had become disintegrated, he could not tell; then, by a sort of instinct, he assumed an erect position, and saw that he was balanced, somehow, a little distance from the bed, looking down upon it. And on the bed, connected with him by a faintly luminous cord, lay the white, still, beautiful form of a dead boy. "And that was my body!" he cried, in awestruck wonder, though his words caused no vibration in the air.

He looked at himself, and saw that he was glorious, encircled by a radiant fire-mist. And he was throbbing and pulsating with life, able to move hither and thither without effort, free from lameness, free from weight, strong, vigorous, full of energy, poised like a bird in the pure air of heaven, ready to take his flight in any conceivable direction at the faintest motion of his own will. Then the resplendence that enveloped him extended, until the whole room was full of it; and in the midst of it there stood a very sweet and gracious figure, robed in white drapery, and with eyes of intensest love, more beautiful to look at than anything that Austin had ever dreamed of. "Mother!" he whispered, as he glided swiftly towards her.

The walls and ceiling of the room dissolved, and a wonderful landscape, the pageantry and splendour of the Spirit Land, revealed itself. It was bathed in a light that never was on land or sea, and there were sunny slopes, and jewelled meadows, and silvery streams, and flowers that only grow in Paradise. Austin was dazzled with its glory; here at last was the realisation of all he had dimly fancied, all he had ever longed for. And yet as he floated outwards and upwards into the heavenly realms, the crown and climax of his happiness lay in the thought that he could always, by the mere impulse of desire, revisit the sweet old garden he had loved, and watch Lubin at his work among the flowers, and stand, though all unseen, beside the old stone fountain where he had passed such happy times in the earth-life he was leaving.

www.ingramcontent.com/pod-product-compliance
Lightning Source LLC
Chambersburg PA
CBHW050756250626
47155CB00005B/2088